BL 4.0
5.0 pt

THE UNGRATEFUL DEAD

ALSO BY ROSE COOPER

The Blogtastic! Novels

Gossip from the Girls' Room

Rumors from the Boys' Room

Secrets from the Sleeping Bag

• • •

I Text Dead People

ROSE COOPER

THE UNGRATEFUL DEAD

DELACORTE PRESS

All rights reserved. Published in the United States by Delacorte Press, an imprint of Random House Children's Books, a division of Penguin Random House LLC, New York.

Delacorte Press is a registered trademark and the colophon is a trademark of Penguin Random House LLC.

randomhousekids.com

Educators and librarians, for a variety of teaching tools, visit us at RHTeachersLibrarians.com

Library of Congress Cataloging-in-Publication Data
Cooper, Rose
Title: The ungrateful dead / Rose Cooper.
Description: First Edition. | New York : Delacorte Press, [2016]
Identifiers: LCCN 2015042021| ISBN 978-0-385-74392-1 (hardback) |
ISBN 978-0-385-37322-7 (ebook)
Subjects: | CYAC: Dead—Fiction. | Future life—Fiction. | Text messages
(Cell phone systems)—Fiction. | BISAC: JUVENILE FICTION / Social Issues /
General (see also headings under Family). | JUVENILE FICTION /
Social Issues / Adolescence.
Classification: LCC PZ7.C78768 Un 2016 | DDC [Fic]—dc23

The text of this book is set in 13-point Chaparral Pro.

Printed in the United States of America
10 9 8 7 6 5 4 3 2 1
First Edition

FOR BRANDON

*I know I don't say it enough, but I'm grateful
to have such an amazing brother.*

CHAPTER 1

ANNA

Annabel Craven stared down at the lifeless body of a girl in her late teens. Her body was still limp and warm, so she hadn't been dead for long. She lay face-down, her neck bent at an awful angle. Her long red hair was clumped to one side. Anna looked up at the balcony the girl had fallen from. Third story, second window from the left.

She knew this because the dead girl was ranting about it.

Well, in her spirit form.

Anna stayed hidden in the shadows, gritting her teeth. It was just her luck that after all these months without any ghostly contact, she just happened to stumble upon this while walking home.

"So much for my almost normal life," Anna mumbled. She knew she had to help this girl. Whether she liked it or not, she was someone who helped bridge the gap between the living and the dead.

Timing was everything, so Anna waited in the shadows while watching the dramatics of the dead girl play out in front of her like a horrible high school production that wasn't worth the five-dollar ticket.

A spirit floated next to the body. "I was just standing on that balcony, for crying out loud!" The dead girl's spirit threw her arms in the air. "One minute I'm there, and the next, I'm . . . here!" she screeched, staring down at her own body lying inches in front of her.

"Look at me! Who did this? Who would've pushed me, Harper Sweety, off that balcony?" the girl wailed. She looked down once more at her body. "Why won't you get up?" she whispered.

Even as a ghost, Harper had style: Her hair flowed symmetrically, spilling red waves over her slim shoulders. She wore a chic black belted dress, cropped jacket, and open-toed gold high heels, looking as if she'd just stepped out of the pages of a fashion magazine. Her lips glowed with glossy pink lipstick, and a luminous glitter trail ran across her dusky eyelids.

Harper had no idea what was happening to her. But Anna knew she couldn't just march right up to her and tell her she was dead. No. Harper had to come to terms with this herself. And then Anna could gently guide—or shove—her in the right direction, depending on how stubborn she was. In fact, she'd started referring to herself as a "Guided."

Going through such a traumatic life-and-death situation could easily cause someone to do silly, if not ridiculous, things.

Anna clamped a hand over her mouth as Harper brushed the pavement with the palms of her hands, sweeping away loose rocks. Then the ghost got down on all fours and lay down on her body.

Harper lay motionless. Her eyes were tightly closed in concentration.

Anna let out a long sigh, her stomach growling. She pulled out her new phone to text her mom.

> Sorry, late for dinner. Lost track of time studying. Be home soon.

She hated lying to her mom, but what was she supposed to say? *Sorry, Mom, late for dinner, this ghost is having body issues?*

Harper's sobs snapped Anna out of her thoughts. There were no tears. Anna had learned ghosts couldn't actually cry, although they could go through the motions.

Harper reached into her left coat pocket and

plucked out her phone. The rhinestone-encrusted case glimmered in the twilight. She angrily punched the buttons as she cried.

Anna's own phone vibrated in her hand. She glanced at the screen. One missed call from a blocked number. Anna shuddered. The last time a blocked number had contacted her, it had been from the dead blowing up her phone. And that hadn't ended well. But that was forever ago. And that was on her old phone. The one she'd buried in the cemetery.

"Okay, let's do this," Anna whispered to herself. She had only taken a few steps before Harper gasped.

"I'm alive!" Harper jumped up and down excitedly as her vacant body started twitching. Anna hated this part. Well, she hated many parts, but this was in the top three. She had to gently break the painfully bad news to Harper that she was not waking up. She was dead. And the twitching was rigor mortis setting in. As Anna skulked over, her sneaker hit a rock and sent it bouncing across the pavement, causing Harper to spin around.

Her hazel eyes were lit with hope as they connected with Anna's dim brown ones. Harper raked her hands down her dress, smoothing out the wrinkles.

"Did you see? Did you?" Harper pointed at her body, speaking excitedly.

Anna definitely wasn't expecting that reaction. She was expecting something more along the lines of "Who are you?" or "What happened?"

"Well, did you?" Harper asked, looking at her impatiently.

Anna had to choose her words carefully now. She had to let Harper down gently. Nothing was worse than traumatizing a ghost right after death. It would be near impossible to help her cross over if that happened.

"You're dead," Anna blurted out before she could stop herself. "For good. As in not coming back, can't reanimate yourself, you're a goner." She said it without expression, in a monotone. It was important not to get emotionally involved in these highly sensitive situations. Anna had learned that the hard way too, not so long ago, when she'd had to deal with her first ghost ever. Lucy had been a ghost in denial (and in love), and only cold hard facts—and a glass coffee table—could help her see the truth.

Anna hoped this worked for all ghosts.

Harper stared wide-eyed at her, speechless. It was a good look for her, Anna thought. But like all good things, it came to an end.

"Oh God. Please do not tell me you're my guardian angel." Harper placed her right hand on her hip, looking Anna up and down. "You have *horrible* fashion sense."

Anna sighed. This girl was worse than a drama queen. Much, much worse.

She was a dead diva. And she smelled like wet socks.

Anna had no choice but to deal with her.

CHAPTER 2

ANNA

Harper let out an exasperated breath, blowing a tendril of hair off her forehead. "Some guardian angel you are! Aren't you supposed to actually save me or something? What were you thinking? Well, apparently you weren't, because I ended up like this."

"Calm down. I'm not an angel," Anna said.

"You can say that again." Harper sat down on her body. "Standing is tiring. Especially in these shoes. And I will *not* get dirt or blood on my dress."

"Clothes should be the least of your worries." Anna couldn't keep the sarcasm from her voice. "And by the way, you're not standing. You're hovering."

"So what am I now exactly—a spirit?"

Before Anna could answer, Harper patted her dead

head. "It was a good body. But if I had known I would only live to be sixteen, I would've eaten more cream puffs. Well, at least I'll look fabulous in my funeral clothes. I hope they fix my neck so my head will be facing the right way." Harper widened her eyes as a sudden thought occurred to her. "My funeral! There is so much planning to do. I have to make sure the right flowers are ordered—lilacs, of course." She tapped her finger on her lips, thinking. "Or maybe white roses. I've always loved white roses. And the guest list. This will take forever. . . ."

"You're not exactly planning a party here, so I'm pretty sure you don't need to stress about the details," Anna said. She forced a smile. "How are you feeling?"

"What are you, my therapist?"

"Do you feel detached or connected to your body? Do you feel weighed down? It makes a difference."

"Seriously? I don't know. I feel weightless, I guess. Like I'm not really here." Harper shrugged. "Whatever. Really, though, I'm just bored out of my mind."

Dead and bored? That was a definite letdown. And apparently all it took was the thought of a party—even if it was a funeral—for Harper to accept the truth.

A streetlamp flickered nearby. It was just after nightfall now, and from the shadows, a homeless man stumbled up to the lamppost and picked up a can, crushing it in his hands before stuffing it in his already overfilled trash bag. The wheels of his cart squeaked as he continued down the road. He never noticed Harper's body.

"Are you kidding me?" Harper shrieked. "He finds a can. Not my *body*, but a freakin' can!"

Harper was still seething when suddenly a woman's scream echoed down the street. Several dogs began barking in the distance. Anna ran back into the shadows, hiding behind a large oak. There was no way she wanted to be implicated in a death. That went way beyond the call of duty.

Harper suddenly stood as the woman ran up to the body and clapped her hand to her mouth. She inched closer to inspect the body.

The woman glanced around, then whipped out a compact from her worn and tattered purse, holding the mirror under Harper's nose. She gasped when the surface didn't fog.

Then the woman stole her shoes.

Harper opened and closed her mouth several times, like a gasping fish out of water, not able to quite work out what had just happened. "You hag!" she screamed after her. Harper stared in shock before finally sighing and sitting back down on top of her lifeless, and now shoeless, body and petting her former head.

Anna's phone vibrated, reminding her of the missed call. And a voice mail. Her eyes widened as she listened to a familiar voice on the message ranting about a pair of Jimmy Choos.

Lucy. The ghost who wouldn't leave her alone.

"No," Anna whispered. "Not again."

CHAPTER 3

Harper

When Harper had opened her eyes, she had blinked frantically until blurry images of her surroundings gradually came into focus. Why was she lying on the floor? No, wait . . . the ground. The dirty, outside ground. She quickly stood up. Electric jolts of panic ran through her.

A body lay on the ground.

Harper gasped, scrambling backward. Then she took a step closer, her skin cold with terror. It was a girl wearing a little black dress. Her face, white as a sheet, had a pinched look. But even in death, she looked fabulous.

Harper recognized that girl.

It was her.

A scream tore from her throat. "That can't be me. It can't be!" Harper looked down at her hands. They were shaking. Her skin was a mind-blowing shade of white that looked as if she hadn't been near a tanning bed in at least a month.

Harper took another shaky step, her legs giving out. As soon as her knees hit the ground, she realized she didn't feel it. In fact, she couldn't feel anything at all. She was completely numb.

"No!" she had shrieked, raking her nails down her arm, leaving wide tracks of red. Still no feeling.

"No, no, no!" She rubbed her arms, trying to erase the marks. But the traces had already vanished.

And now here she was.

. . .

Anna had given Harper only two options:

1. Follow Anna back to Maddsen Manor—
   Anna's house had a *name*—and let Anna
   "help" her. Which probably meant listen to
   her lectures until Harper went screaming
   over to the other side just to get away
   from her.
2. Not follow Anna back to her house and
   deal with everything on her own.

The thought of following Anna was about as appealing as getting poison oak and chicken pox at the same time. But really, what else could she do? If she didn't stay with Anna tonight she'd have to hang out here all by herself, with the dark woods looming close by.

A cold shock ran through Harper as she was seized again with the terrible realization: She was dead. *What does someone do after they die? Where do they go?* Would she wander around aimlessly forever, in a state of limbo? And was this tiny town of Winchester Village considered limbo?

Out of habit, Harper inhaled a deep breath and slowly let it out.

Her eyes slid along the tree line. Anna had moved away from her and was busy texting. She wasn't paying attention to Harper.

And that's when Harper noticed the *other* girl.

A girl. Standing several feet away. Wearing mismatched clothes and probably close to Harper's age.

The girl raised a hand at Harper before flipping her hair over one shoulder.

She can see me? Harper thought, surprised.

As the girl moved closer, Harper noticed her shoes were fabulous. And her skin was eerily translucent. Harper could see the trees right through her back. A strange incandescent light radiated from her, illuminating her from the inside like a jack-o'-lantern.

"Who are you?" Harper's voice shook.

The girl looked Harper up and down. "I've been waiting for you. Dying to meet you, actually."

The girl glanced at the body lying on the ground.

"Waiting?" Harper's eyes widened. "Oh my God . . . you're the one who killed me!"

The girl rolled her eyes. "Please. I have no reason to kill. Unless, of course, you go after my boyfriend. But let's not go there."

"So who are you, then? Are you like Anna? Or are—"

"Shhh! Not so loud!" The girl looked over at Anna, who was frowning at her phone and tapping at the screen. "The last thing we need is Anna to hear us and come running back. I'm Lucy Edwards, and I'm nothing like Anna."

"But you know her?"

"Of course. She tried to steal my boyfriend while trying to get me to cross over to the other side."

"Cross over? You mean you're . . . a spirit?"

Lucy folded her arms across her chest, looking irritated. "Um, think about it. Are normal people able to float? Can you see through people if they aren't spirits? It's common sense, really."

Harper looked down to see Lucy hovering only an inch or so above the ground. "You call that floating? I can jump higher than that in my heels." Harper quickly shut her mouth as she saw anger flash over Lucy's face.

"So, um . . . you didn't cross over, though?"

"Let's just say it's complicated."

"Well, I don't want to cross over." Harper's eyes widened. "Are those the clothes you died in?"

Lucy laughed. "Seriously?"

"Well . . . yeah. I mean, you were either in a horrible accident with a washing machine, or death is cruel in the afterlife. In which case, I'm really not doing that crossing-over thing."

Lucy smiled. "I was hoping you'd say that. Being dead isn't as great as you'd think, am I right?"

Harper was silent for a moment. Nothing about being dead sounded great.

"So what if you didn't have to stay dead?" Lucy asked slyly.

Harper peeked sideways at Lucy. "As in . . . I could be alive again?"

"Yep. What if I told you you could get your body back?"

Harper paused. There had to be a catch. There was always a catch. "What's in it for you?"

Lucy shrugged. "Can't I just help a girl out without expecting something in return?"

Harper hesitated. "I've never done that for anybody.

So I guess it seems weird that a total stranger would do something like that for me."

"Well, you *might* be able to help me out with something once you're part of the living again."

Harper nodded. She knew there had to be something behind Lucy's offer. "Help with what, exactly?"

"Nah-ah," Lucy said, wagging her finger, her voice scolding. "First you get your body, then we'll talk."

If Harper could rejoin the living, maybe she could sell her story, make it into a reality show, even! She thought of all the YouTube and Instagram personalities she followed. Sure, they had fame and fortune, but none of them had a story like this. This made her special. And it could make her rich. Popular. And extremely famous. What dead girl wouldn't want that?

"Deal," Harper agreed.

CHAPTER 4

ANNA

Anna groaned as another message popped up on her iPad. She had left Harper in the woods yesterday. But she hadn't been able to stop thinking about her all day at school today. And now she was back at her house, getting messages from her. "They're baaaack."

"Ghosts?" Anna's friend Eden Ashbury looked up from the faux-fur beanbag she was lounging in on the floor. "They're contacting you again?"

"Uh-huh. And remember when I told you about that Harper girl yesterday?"

"Yeah."

"Well, after I left her, I started getting text messages again." She rolled over on her bed, making the old black iron bed frame creak. She held up her iPad so Eden could see the screen.

This is so weird.

Forests are creepy.

I'm not sure what to dooooooooooo?

Yo

Anna?

Are you there???????

"It's so weird that it's happening again," Eden said. "You buried your old phone, didn't you?"

Anna nodded. But burying the phone hadn't buried the problem. "Maybe this Harper girl did something to establish another connection with me. Maybe, somehow, my ability went viral in the spirit world." She sighed, tossing her iPad on her bed. "All it took was one ghost to say, 'Hey, Anna got a new phone! Now we can contact her again. And use her iPad too. That will really annoy her.'"

"They probably aren't trying to annoy you," Eden said. "They just need help and you're someone who can help them."

"I'm not so sure about that," Anna mumbled.

"It definitely sucks," Eden said. "I would hate getting bugged all the time by ghosts. But you're not the only one having phone trouble." She shook her phone furiously. "Stupid thing. Never works when it's supposed to."

"You know what will happen if you shake your phone even harder?" Anna asked.

"What?" Eden said, shaking it harder.

"Nothing." Anna giggled.

"Ha-ha, very funny." Eden tossed her phone aside on the plush purple rug in Anna's room. "I'm about ready to throw it at the wall."

Anna couldn't help but laugh at how quickly Eden had gotten frustrated. Usually she was so calm and could handle any situation. Apparently phones were the one thing that really got to her. "What are you even looking for?"

"I need a specific spell for something . . . well, specific."

"And I'm guessing that you're not going to tell me what specifically it is?" Anna raised an eyebrow.

"Not yet. But I will." Eden retrieved her phone and turned it off, then on again.

If anyone had told Anna a few months ago she would become friends with one of the Ashbury twins, she would've laughed. And if anyone had told her Eden was a witch, well, Anna might just have died from laughter.

Anna and her mom had inherited Maddsen Manor from her mom's uncle. At the time, Anna had thought that leaving behind their old, cramped one-bedroom apartment and the bad luck that always seemed to follow them was like winning the lottery.

She hadn't realized that their fresh start would involve communicating with dead people.

Thankfully, Eden was very much alive. Surprisingly, she was a witch.

Eden wasn't a dark witch, though. She didn't have a wart on her nose or ride around on a broom. She also wasn't a good witch who wore fluffy dresses and helped people with a sparkly wand or fairy dust. She was the kind of witch who looked like a Barbie doll, lived in a mansion, kept her witchcraft a secret, and had an evil identical twin named Olivia.

Eden scrolled through her apps. "Aha! I think I found it!"

When Anna first learned that Eden was a witch, she expected her to have a huge black book, the cover barely hanging on and the pages yellowed with age, containing spells and witchcraft passed down for generations. Wasn't that how witches operated? But apparently, modern-day witches were way past that. They had Spell Phones.

Eden's phone had apps exclusively for witches and a link to an app store, where they could purchase additional spells. There were even meet-ups for witches in the area, but Eden refused to say if there was anyone like her at their school, Winchester Academy. "The people who know about us are limited," she had told Anna. "We are very selective. Not even Olivia knows the truth. It's just better that way."

"But she's your twin, Eden. How is that possible?" Anna couldn't imagine having a sister, let alone keeping such an incredible secret from her.

Eden had shrugged. "That's just how it is. But it's not something I can ignore about myself. Ignoring it is just dangerous."

"Tell me about it," Anna had mumbled. She had tried ignoring all the texts she received from dead people, but that made it worse. Much worse. She'd quickly learned that spirits didn't like to be ignored. That made them mad.

The sooner she could get them to stop showing up and interrupting her life, the better, she thought now. If only she could figure out how to do that.

"Why did you trust me so quickly?" Anna asked.

"You're different. And once I knew you could

communicate with ghosts, I figured you'd understand and not run blabbing to the whole school."

Anna smiled. Eden had caught her in mid-conversation with a ghost. She had had to either tell her the truth or look like a crazy person.

Since they'd started hanging out, Anna realized the witch stuff wasn't as bad as she'd thought. And despite appearances, Eden was nothing at all like Olivia.

"Have you ever thought of doing a niceness spell on Olivia?" Anna asked.

"I have!" Eden's eyes widened in seriousness. "I did a Sugar and Spice spell, but it didn't really work. She acted even worse, if you can believe it. Bad side effects."

"Side effects?" Anna repeated.

"Oh yeah, every spell has a side effect. Think of it as being like medication. Some people can have a bad reaction, and some can feel side effects worse than others. It's just the probability is greater when you're doing a spell that has a high degree of difficulty."

Anna thought about this. "So what you're saying is that Olivia isn't capable of ever being nice."

Eden looked sad. "Not if she doesn't get something out of it."

"I'm so glad you broke away from her and her group."

"Me too. It was scary but it was worth it. I couldn't

have done it if it weren't for you." She smiled at Anna. "You're my sister from another mister."

Anna smiled back. "Don't start getting all mushy on me, now."

Laughing, Eden grabbed a pillow near her and threw it at Anna.

Although Eden was quickly becoming Anna's best friend, Anna still thought often of Millie. Millie, aka Millicent Marguerite Maddsen, her best friend and great-aunt and a ghost. Millie had died in 1947, but she had lived for decades in denial about what had happened to her. It was a long, sad story. At last, with Anna's help, she had accepted her fate. She hadn't been ready to move on, and Anna hadn't been ready to say goodbye.

But she had moved on. And Anna had been forced to say goodbye.

Ever since, Anna had felt lonely. She told herself she needed to make new friends. Human friends. And luckily, she and Eden had grown close. But still, every once in a while, she would talk out loud, hoping Millie would hear her if she was around.

Deep in her heart, Anna knew Millie would find a way to contact her again.

Millie was a ghost she *wanted* to hear from. She had so many things she wanted to tell her. Three things, to be exact.

1. They had been wrong about Eden. She was nothing like Olivia. And she had stopped allowing Olivia to take over her life.
2. Johnny. Johnny, Johnny, Johnny. Anna loved how the name of her crush rolled off her tongue. Poor Johnny. A few months ago, that pain-in-the-neck ghost Lucy had managed to take over Eden's body. Lucy-as-Eden had pushed Johnny through Anna's living room glass-top table (OUCH!). Luckily, he was okay. But he had lost any memories from that night and the months before the accident. Memories that included Anna (OUCH!). When Anna's mom came home, she assumed the blonde was Olivia, not Eden, and Anna never corrected her. Especially since Eden didn't remember anything either after she got her body back.
3. Millie was right. The whole popularity thing *was* overrated. And since she'd figured that out, her life was much better. Anna would rather have a few great friends than a ton of okay friends who were all about the drama and backstabbing.

The girls walked down to Anna's kitchen to get something to eat. Anna put on the teakettle and took out some mugs from the kitchen cabinet. "I wish Johnny could just remember me from before the accident." She rummaged around the cabinet and found a box of chocolate chip cookies. "It would make life so much easier. I hate this starting-over thing."

"Maybe it's not so bad," Eden said. "This way, you can start out fresh."

"Yeah. Maybe." But Johnny wasn't the only one who had lost his memories. When Lucy supposedly crossed over to the other side and gave Eden her body back, Eden didn't remember a single thing about what had gone down. She didn't even know she was there when it happened. Anna didn't want to tell her, because she knew Eden would feel responsible.

"Hey, check out this spell!" Eden said suddenly as she stopped scrolling on her phone. "I could whip something up to help Johnny remember you."

"Whip something up?" Anna repeated.

"Yeah, I could make a memory cake." Eden made it sound like altering someone's memories was normal.

"Memory cake?"

"Are you just going to repeat everything I say?"

"Repeat everything?" Anna said, giggling.

Eden groaned. "Okay, I know you do that whenever you're trying to avoid something, but look, what would be so wrong with me giving Johnny back something he lost?"

"I've tasted your cooking before, Eden. I don't think poisoning him would help."

"Shut up!" Eden laughed. "As long as I follow this recipe, it would be safe."

"Yeahhhh, I don't know. What if it did the opposite? Like removed his memories from the last few weeks? That's the last thing I need."

Eden shook her head. "No, it doesn't work like that. Worst case, nothing would happen and his memory loss would stay the same. The side effects would be minimal, if there were any at all. Now, if I gave it to someone who didn't have any lost memories, that'd be a whole other story."

"Spells can go wrong, though," Anna pointed out, feeling a little nervous about the whole thing. Just then the teakettle started to boil, its whistle piercing.

"True, but not in the way you're thinking. It sounds like you're just making up excuses."

That was exactly what she was doing. She really wanted Johnny to get his memories back, but that also meant he would know the truth about that night. And there were certain things that were better left forgotten.

"At least think about it?"

Anna nodded. "Okay." But thinking about something is totally different from doing something.

CHAPTER 5

Harper

Harper and Lucy were in the middle of a ghost-to-ghost tutorial, and it was not going well.

At all.

"So how am I supposed to get back into my body?" Harper demanded, her voice shrill. She stared down at the fresh mound of dirt at her feet. "Especially since it was *buried* this morning?"

Lucy let out a loud sigh. "Calm down. Like I keep telling you, you just sink into the ground and into your body."

"But *I* told *you* that didn't work the first five times I tried, so why would it suddenly work now?" She felt the need to blink back imaginary tears. Standing in the middle of a deserted cemetery, staring out at moss-covered urns and headstones of long-forgotten people, was not how she wanted to spend her morning.

Or her afternoon.

Or her evening.

But she didn't have anything else to do, or anyplace else to go. She blinked faster.

"Again, Harper. Like I keep telling you. You're a spirit now. You gain strength every moment you stay in this form."

Harper glanced down at her phone. "It's been four days, sixteen hours, and twenty-eight minutes. I can't be that much more powerful."

"Yes, you can. Trust me, you're definitely powerful enough to do this simple task."

Harper sniffed. "How can you be so sure this will work? And what if I do get back inside my body and I'm trapped? Underground? And then I'm buried alive?" She felt her dead heart speed up.

"You're already dead," Lucy reminded her, which was totally unnecessary. "You can't be buried alive. And you won't be trapped. Your strength from your current form will transfer with you into your body. You have a small window of time to use that power before your energy is absorbed and you're only as strong as your actual body."

"But how do you know this will work?" Harper asked meekly.

"Because I know," Lucy barked. "Stop questioning me."

"You've never done this before, have you?" Harper asked.

"Well, define 'never,'" Lucy said.

"You are infuriating!"

"Look, I met this guy named Rick on the other side and he taught me some tricks to this spirit stuff," Lucy said. "This is one of them. Try it again."

Harper didn't want to try it again. But as she looked around at the wilted flowers and gravestones, she realized that trying again was the only thing she had left.

CHAPTER 6

ANNA

Anna watched Johnny and Spencer play air hockey while she sat on a couch nearby. The clubhouse next to the public swimming pool was *the* hangout spot in the village. And luckily, it wasn't too far a walk from Maddsen Manor. Anna scrolled through the messages on her phone. She had a text from Eden.

Running late. Be there in a few.

When Anna looked back up, Johnny was gone and Spencer was playing against someone else.

"Hey, Anna." Johnny sat down next to her, startling her.

She jumped a little but hoped he hadn't noticed. "Hey."

"Want a soda?" He held up a Coke bottle.

"Um, sure. Thanks," she said, taking the bottle from him. Being here with him, in this moment, reminded her of something. "Remember that one time when—" She cut herself off. Of course he didn't remember. He'd lost all his memories! She looked up at Johnny. "Sorry. I didn't mean—"

"Don't worry about it," he said, running his fingers through his hair. "Happens all the time."

Another thing she loved about Johnny: He was so easygoing. Oh, and the way he pushed his hair out of his face like that. And when he bit the corner of his bottom lip when he was thinking. And—oh, he was saying something to her. "I'm sorry, what did you just say?"

Johnny laughed. "If I'm boring you, just let me know."

"You could never bore me," she said, a little more enthusiastically than she probably should have. She could feel her cheeks turn red.

"So tell me about it."

Anna's hand reached up to her cheek. "Huh?"

"Tell me what you were going to say. About what you remember. You never know. It might help me remember too."

After the last few months of doing this, Anna knew he wouldn't, but she usually went along with it anyway. But not this time. Because this time it involved certain secrets that he didn't remember about her.

And that was the hardest to deal with. The doctor had said his memory loss was probably just temporary. Anna's mom told her to think positive and just look at it like a fresh start. That was exactly what Anna *didn't* want.

She hadn't had much luck with fresh starts.

But now, the more time she spent with Johnny, the stronger her feelings for him got. And she had no idea what he really thought of her.

"Nah," Anna said, dismissing the idea. "It wasn't anything interesting."

"Oh. Well, okay then." He smiled at her and she practically melted. His dimples were so cute.

Just then Eden walked into the clubhouse, and Anna couldn't help but wonder: What if Eden was right? What if her friend's memory cake could help Johnny after all?

Johnny went to hang out with some of the guys from his football team and Eden took his spot beside Anna.

"What's up?" Eden asked, dropping her backpack on the ground.

"Nothing," she said, taking a swig of her soda. "The

same. Mom is always gone. She quit her job at Twisted and went full-time at the funeral home. So she's either working or with Winston. Same thing, really."

"Oh, *that's* not creepy."

"Right?"

"Did she do that after the wedding?"

"Yeah. Like practically the next day."

Anna's mom had had what some might call a whirlwind romance with Winston Doombrowski, the mortician at the funeral home. Anna thought it was ridiculous. Sure, all she had ever wanted was for her mom to be happy. But Anna had shoes that she had had longer than her mom had known Winston. It was like they met, got engaged, and married practically on the first date.

"I read that people who fall in love fast stay together longer than people who date forever," Eden said. "You never know."

"It's just weird," Anna said. "One day he's just Mr. Doom, our neighbor and the town's funeral director, and the next day he and his fuzzy black mustache are living in the Manor with us and recruiting Mom as a corpse cosmetologist."

Eden wrinkled her nose. "Yeah, I can see how that would feel strange. But isn't it kind of nice to have a stepdad? I mean, you and your mom were alone in

Maddsen Manor for a while . . . isn't it nice to have somebody else there with you?"

Anna's real father had passed away when she was little, so it had always been just her and her mom. She'd never thought too much about having a step-father. But now that she had one, it wasn't exactly a dream come true. It kind of felt like her mom and Winston were a team and she was just a third wheel.

"Eh. It's not so great." Anna shrugged. "He pretty much acts like he's in charge now, even though he's only lived there for a second."

"I think that's normal."

"Maybe. But now I have a schedule I have to follow. Like, what does it matter if I want to do my homework before dinner or after, you know?"

Eden patted her on the arm. "Weird. I'm glad I don't have to deal with any of that."

"Thanks for the support."

"You know I'm here if you need me."

"Can you whip up a vanishing spell?"

"For you? Or Winston?"

CHAPTER 7

Harper

As Lucy had instructed, Harper had knelt at her grave and envisioned her body just below the surface. Well, six feet below. She closed her eyes and lay on her grave faceup, her feet planted firmly against her headstone.

It felt like walking through walls. She felt herself sinking down. Farther and farther, as if she were sinking into one of those super-comfortable mattresses they had at that store at the mall. Except it went on forever. She concentrated and imagined herself in her body.

Then blackness.

A soft glow shone through her closed lids. Her eyes launched open. She felt something solid. Reflexively she parted her lips to scream before realizing that it had happened.

She was back in her body.

Her body! She was doing it! Except . . . something was off. Her body was backward! Her hands were down by her feet. Who had buried her backward? How could they do this to her?

"Okay, just concentrate, Harpie," she said, talking herself down, turning herself to face the other way until she felt her hands actually moving. Her hands! She wiggled her fingers. She had actual fingers! And feet. And . . . Oomph! She hit her head on the lid of the coffin as she tried to sit up.

Pain. She'd almost forgotten what it felt like to feel pain.

Panic seized Harper. Now that she was back in her body, she had a new problem: she was buried alive! Her worst fear. Actually, it was her second-worst fear. Her first was a recurring nightmare she had: her credit card being cut in front of the whole store of shoppers while she was trying to purchase the latest must-have purse. The most embarrassing moment ever.

"Okay, think," Harper whispered to herself. "What did Lucy say next? To focus, right?" Her strength would be gone in just a few minutes. She had to act fast. Now or never. And she never settled for never.

She summoned all her strength. Placing both hands palm side up on the top while kicking with both legs, she gave it everything she had. "Oomph!"

And then she did it again. The flimsy coffin lid opened and dirt fell on top of her. "I guess my family didn't pay for the deluxe coffin," she mumbled. But who cared, really? She was doing this!

She clawed her way through the dirt, pulling herself up into the open air and onto the ground.

She was free! And she was alive again! She examined her arms and legs as if she were just feeling her body for the first time. Harper looked around. Where was Lucy? There was no sign of her. She'd promised she would be there in case Harper needed her.

But off in the distance, someone was there. Someone who shouldn't have been. Had that person seen everything?

Harper squinted. Maybe her eyes were just playing tricks on her. Or was someone really there watching her?

The cemetery was bathed in shadows. Harper decided she was just a little rattled. Her eyes probably were still adjusting to, well, being eyes again. She blinked rapidly. She'd have to pick up some eyedrops at the pharmacy.

Harper walked as fast as she could toward what

she hoped was the exit. But for her, fast was a relative term. Her body felt stiff and robotic, and she moved with a slight limp.

If someone was really there watching her, it would be a big problem. Because if anyone saw her and told her secret, her second chance at life would be very short-lived. And Harper couldn't let that happen.

CHAPTER 8

ANNA

Anna rubbed her eyes. She saw a lot of things most people couldn't see. And in this case, it was the dead girl, Harper. Standing at her front door. Wearing the black belted dress and cropped jacket.

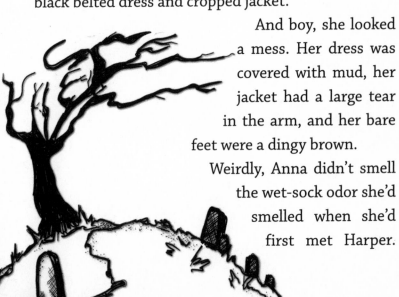

And boy, she looked a mess. Her dress was covered with mud, her jacket had a large tear in the arm, and her bare feet were a dingy brown.

Weirdly, Anna didn't smell the wet-sock odor she'd smelled when she'd first met Harper.

Each spirit she had known had a different, distinct smell.

The only thing Anna smelled right now was dirt.

"Um, hey." Anna didn't know where to start.

"Hi," Eden said from behind her.

Anna spun around. Eden was looking right at Harper. "You can see her?"

Eden nodded. "Yep!"

Anna elbowed Eden in the side and whispered, "*That* is *Harper*."

"Harper?" Eden's eyes widened. "As in dead Harper?"

Anna nodded, staring at Harper. As if she might just disappear if she took her eyes off her for a moment.

"Wait a minute . . ." Eden trailed off, turning to Anna. "If I can see her, then . . . I see dead people?"

"Would you stop?" Harper threw her hands in the air. "Sorry to burst your bubble, but I am *not* dead."

"I think this one is in denial too," Eden whispered to Anna.

"I'm not in denial, because I'm not dead!" Harper said, her voice rising.

"I thought you understood all this," Anna said with a sigh. "And since you're here, I'm guessing that trying to deal with everything on your own didn't work out so well, and that you came to my house to ask for my help."

Harper stood with her hands on her hips, annoyed. "Look, I don't need anything from you." Then she hesitated. "Well, that's not entirely true. I do need something from you. I just don't need your lectures."

"Come in," Anna said, waving her through the entryway. She, Eden, and Harper went into the living room. Anna and Eden sat on the couch. Harper sat on a chair, facing them.

If Anna hadn't been so curious about Harper's new living status, she would've thrown her butt out.

"Okay, so tell us everything," Anna said. "How did this happen?"

"I met your friend Lucy."

Anna shook her head. "No. No, that's not possible."

"For a girl who can see ghosts, you really think a lot of things are impossible," Harper said.

Anna sighed. "What I mean is that Lucy—who really wasn't my friend—is dead, and her spirit moved on. So whoever you met, it couldn't have been Lucy."

"Really? Because this girl was dead. Is dead. And I'm guessing you're not friends because *you* tried to steal *her* boyfriend," Harper said. "At least, that's what she told me."

"Oooh, that does sound like Lucy," Eden said.

"I did not steal her boyfriend!" Anna said, exasperated. She took a deep breath. "How, exactly, did she

41

help you? How did you come back to life and start breathing again?"

Harper pursed her lips, as if she was thinking about how to best say this. "Technically, my body is dead."

Anna and Eden shared a look

"My body was already buried but my spirit simply took over again," Harper went on, giving a small shrug. "At least, that's what I think happened."

"So how does Lucy fit into all this?" Anna asked. "I mean, assuming that you had contact with the *real* Lucy."

"She made me realize my powers and how to use them," Harper said. "That's all."

"Let me get this straight." Anna let out a huge sigh she hadn't realized she was holding in. "Lucy is back. As in here? In town?"

Harper nodded. "That's what I said, isn't it?"

"This is so not good," Anna mumbled to herself. She turned to Eden. "But I don't get it. Lucy moved on. Or at least I thought she did. She said she was."

"And you believed her?" Eden asked.

"I guess I just wanted her gone so bad I took her word for it," Anna said morosely. "But why would she be back?"

"Didn't you say you thought she might come back someday?"

"Yeah, someday. Not this soon. She must be up to something."

Anna looked out the window, letting this news sink in. When she'd first moved to town and found a phone in the woods, she'd never imagined that it would lead to texts from dead people . . . or actual dead people turning up at her house. She watched a car drive slowly past the gate to her house.

Was there a ghost driving it?

Or a zombie?

Was she doomed to a life where nothing would ever be normal again?

"Anna!" Eden snapped her fingers in front of Anna's face, startling her. "Are you there? You've been staring out that window forever."

"Yeah, hello? Can we focus on me and my problem?" Harper snapped.

Anna nodded. "Sorry. It just—all this"—she waved her hand in Harper's direction—"it got to me."

Eden shrugged. "I don't get what the big deal is. Harper's being, uh, *back* won't affect anybody."

Anna gaped at her. "Are you kidding? What about her family? Her friends? You don't think they'll freak when they see her walking around again?" Clearly Eden hadn't thought this whole thing through.

Anna's mind was spinning at the horror of it all.

"I'll stay here," Harper blurted out. "In the village. And I'll change schools. It's not likely anyone I know will ever see me."

"Of course it's likely," Anna pointed out, trying not to roll her eyes. "You didn't live that far from here when you were, um, alive."

Harper stared blankly at her.

"You know, that apartment I found you at," Anna prompted. "It's pretty close to my house."

"That run-down dump?" Harper snorted. "I didn't live there. I was . . . visiting."

"Visiting? Visiting who?" Anna asked.

"That doesn't matter," Harper said quickly. "More important is this: have you figured out who pushed me off that balcony?"

Anna shook her head. "But to be honest, I haven't actually been trying to solve that mystery." She looked over at Eden and then met Harper's gaze directly. "And how do we know you were really pushed? I'm beginning to think you just somehow randomly tripped over your own feet and fell."

Harper crossed her arms. "You know I was pushed because I'm telling you that's what happened and I'm not a liar. Besides, I know what a push feels like. And look at me. Once I take a shower and put on some clean clothes, I won't be any different from anyone else. No one around here will know me, so guess what? Problem solved."

"She has a point, Anna," Eden said.

A wave of uneasiness fell over Anna. "I don't like this," she said finally. "It's not safe. I just know something bad will happen."

"Aw, lighten up, Anna," Eden said, picking up her phone and checking her texts. "You're being kind of paranoid. If Harper's back, she's back, and it's not really up to you to judge, is it?" She tilted her head up toward the fireplace mantel, where the wedding picture of Anna's mom and Winston sat in a big shiny frame. "You're kind of sounding like your mom, you know?"

Harper laughed. "Yeah. Don't get all nervous. It's not like I could die again."

Anna picked up one of the new embroidered pillows her mom had received as a wedding gift and hugged it to her chest. This was so not how she wanted to spend her day.

"I hate to state the obvious, guys, but here it is," Harper said. "I need a place to stay."

"I guess you do," Anna said slowly, wondering where this was going to go. *Nowhere good,* a little voice told her.

"I can't go back to my house, for obvious reasons,"

Harper said, raising an eyebrow. She spread her arms out wide. "This is certainly a big house you have here."

Anna shook her head. A boulder rested in the pit of her stomach.

"No. Way."

Harper gave her a strained smile. "Okay, guess I'm going back home, then. I'll be sure to mention your name to the media. See ya, girls." She swiveled on her muddy heel and walked toward the front door.

"You can't let her go back," Eden said. "People can't find out about stuff like this. The whole town will freak. Other secrets will eventually be exposed."

Like Eden's secret, Anna thought.

"Well, what am I supposed to do?" Anna asked, feeling a wave of panic. "I can't exactly let her live here at Maddsen Manor! My mom would never allow it."

"Your mom doesn't have to know."

Anna's mouth dropped open. "Are you kidding me? My mom always finds stuff out."

"Does she know you're a Guided?"

Anna shrugged. "I'm sure she will. . . . It's only a matter of time. Plus, Winston is living here now too."

"Your house is huge, though. And Winston is hardly ever home. There's really not a big chance he or your mom will run into Harper if you guys are careful about it. Harper could just be your friend hanging out after school, and then at night you could sneak her into one of the rooms that your mom doesn't use."

Anna bit her lip. It was true—the house was huge. There were rooms that they had never even gone into since they'd moved here from their cramped one-bedroom apartment.

"It's so big!" Anna had said when they'd walked down the long hallways.

"So much to take care of," her mom had said. Ultimately her mom had decided to use only certain rooms as actual living space, closing the doors to the other rooms and halls. "Keep the doors closed," she'd said to Anna. "Otherwise our heating bill is going to be insane."

"But if she moves in here, there's no way I'm going to hang around with her every day," Anna said now, feeling miserable about the whole thing.

Eden shrugged. "Then don't. Just find a way she can sneak in. This is a super-old house. Are there any hidden entrances?"

Anna thought for a moment. "Not that I know of."

"In a mansion built in the eighteen hundreds, my guess is that there are some secrets you still haven't discovered. If we can find a secret entrance, we find the answer to your problem."

Anna wasn't so sure. "But what if Harper's secret *does* get out?"

"You aren't going to say anything. I'm not going to say anything. I'm pretty sure she isn't either," Eden said.

"Okay." Anna sighed. "I guess I better go after Harper and hope I can find her in time."

"No need, I'm right here!" Harper poked her head around the doorway and smiled. "I knew you'd come to your senses."

CHAPTER 9

ANNA

"So, great news!" her mom said brightly, taking a left onto Brightwood Avenue. Anna and her mom were on their way to the grocery store. Her mom wanted to make something special for Winston for dinner that night.

"I hate when you say that, Mom," Anna said dully. "Last time you gave me great news, we moved . . . *here.*"

Her mom chuckled. "I'll pretend you didn't just say that. I'm glad you're sitting down."

"Me too. I mean, since we're in a car and everything," Anna said, waiting for her mom to share whatever this great news was. Experience had taught her that she and her mom didn't have the same criteria for "great."

"You have a stepsister!" her mom blurted out.

Anna's mouth dropped open. She squeezed the armrest tight. "How is that possible? Winston doesn't have any kids." She thought back to the wedding. Nope, no kids. She'd been the youngest person there by about thirty years.

"Actually, he does," her mom said, shooting a glance over at Anna.

Anna let out a loud groan. "Did you *know* he had kids, Mom?"

"Well, not exactly. I mean, I knew he was married before but . . ." Her voice trailed off.

"Don't you think that's kind of weird, though?" Anna asked, her eyes narrowing. "That he never told you?"

Her mom came to a stop at a light. "I'm sure he has reasons for it."

"She didn't even come to the wedding!"

"I know, but she was having problems accepting her parents' divorce," her mom said in the patient voice she always used when dealing with an unpleasant situation. "She's acted out a lot. What she needs now is a family. *Our* family."

Anna rolled her eyes. Her lovesick mom would forever be making excuses whenever it came to Winston. In her eyes, he was perfect.

"So, where is his daughter?" Anna had always wanted a sister. Maybe it wouldn't be that bad.

"She's been bouncing back and forth between her parents. Winston sent her to live with her mom in Manhattan right before we moved here, actually. But now she's moving back."

"He sent her to New York City? Why?"

"I guess she got into a bit of trouble and it was too much for him to handle on his own. I don't know what exactly happened, but it sounds like she's changed. For the better."

"How much can one person change in less than a year?" Anna pointed out.

"Let's just give her a chance, okay?" her mom asked.

"Yes, of course, Mom." She let out a long sigh. If that was what it took to make her mom happy.

Now that the news was out, her mom couldn't stop smiling. "Her name is Tabitha. She's only a year older than you. Isn't that great?"

Anna forced a smile. "Wonderful." The whole Harper situation had just gotten a bit trickier. But maybe it wouldn't be as bad as she thought. It could be awesome having someone here around her age.

"And don't worry, even though she went to your school for a short time before, I'm sure it will be fine. This will be a fresh start for her." Anna's mom beamed her snow-white teeth. She knew how to radiate a smile. How could Anna not be happy? "I was thinking I'd make a vegetarian lasagna. I'll buy a jar of that fancy marinara you like, and we'll get some of those fresh noodles they sell in the deli case. . . ."

Anna traced her finger down the window, staring out at the highway, seeing nothing. "Perfect." She was already mortified to be forcibly associated with death. Permanently. She had become an undertaker's stepdaughter, and now she would be linked to a girl known for causing problems.

It scared Anna on some level, knowing everything was about to change for the hundredth time.

And life as she knew it would never be the same again.

• • •

Eden swung her legs as she sat next to Anna on the Manor's porch swing. "So let me get this straight. Your mom just told you that you have a stepsister."

Anna had texted Eden with a 911 as soon as she got home and finished helping her mom carry in all the grocery bags.

Anna nodded. "It's true."

"Seriously?" Eden's eyes widened.

"Yeah. Winston has a daughter around our age. She lives with her mom on the East Coast, and not even my mom knew about her until now. But she's moving back here and into the Manor and will be going to our school." She blurted the terrible news out fast, like ripping off a Band-Aid.

"Whoa! Who knew the creepy undertaker had any kids."

"Right. But did you hear the part about her moving in?" Anna said glumly. "As in *here*. In *this* house. Where I'm secretly going to be helping *and* hiding from a, well, whatever Harper is."

"Don't worry. I already told you I'm helping with that." Eden placed her hand on Anna's arm.

Anna felt a weird calming sensation take over. All her muscles instantly relaxed; the tension drained from her body. And her head cleared from the fog of questions that had clouded her mind only seconds before.

"How'd you do that?"

"It's one of my gifts." Eden smiled.

"You mean one of your spells? Is that why you're usually calm?"

Eden nodded. "What kind of friend would I be if I didn't share?"

"I'm afraid to even ask what other spells you might have done on me."

"I would never secretly do something to you." Eden looked hurt.

"I know. I was just kidding," Anna told her, then thought, *Kind of.* She continued, "So this girl, Tabitha. She was living with her mom but—"

Eden interrupted her. "Why does that name sound familiar?"

"Maybe you met her? She lived her for a few months. Before I moved here. She changed her last name when her mom did after the divorce, back to her mom's maiden name. Not that I could blame her for not wanting to be Doombrowski."

"It's not Tabitha Richland, is it?"

"Yeah."

"You know her?"

"Know her? Everyone knows her. She wasn't here that long, but definitely long enough to leave an impression."

"What kind of impression?"

"Let's just say she found her way to becoming top cheerleader, going over Olivia's head."

"So she and Olivia weren't friends."

"No, they were best friends. Until Tabitha back-stabbed her."

Anna smiled. "She can't be that bad then, if she backstabbed Olivia."

"She's worse."

"Worse?" Anna repeated.

"Yes. She's even more ruthless than my sister. And when she wants something, she will stop at nothing."

"Great. And now she'll be living with me."

"No one ever knew her dad was the undertaker. Having a different last name probably made it easy for her to keep it a secret."

"I guess we're not the only ones who keep secrets," Anna whispered.

"We definitely aren't. Everyone here has secrets. The smaller the town, the bigger the secrets. And trust me, nothing ever stays buried forever here."

CHAPTER 10

ANNA

Anna expected Tabitha to look like Olivia and her clones. To be tall and flawless, tan and blond. To carry herself in a way that told everyone else she was better than they were. Anna expected to be intimidated by her new stepsister.

But she was just the opposite.

Tabitha reminded Anna of a doll she used to play with when she was a kid, one of a collection. She was tiny, with the same perfect features. Her hair was as black as a raven, contrasting with her snow-white skin. She wore jeans and a tee, much like Anna. And she was quiet.

Anna's mom made her stay home that weekend and spend her time helping Tabitha unpack. *Nobody ever helped me unpack*, Anna thought.

Tabitha ignored her. She didn't seem to need any help unpacking anything, and anything Anna did put away for her—her sneakers in the shoe closet, her shampoo bottles in the bathroom—Tabitha ended up taking out and putting back herself. Not once did they say anything to each other. The only ones who talked were Winston and her mom, when they came to check on their progress. Actually, Anna was the only one making progress. Tabitha spent an hour looking at every item she took out of her suitcases and some boxes her mom had shipped as if she hadn't seen it for years and needed to remember its special sentimental significance before she could even think about putting it away.

Anna's phone vibrated in her pocket.

Hey you! Wanna meet at the clubhouse later?

It was from Eden. Anna's heart soared when she saw a text from Johnny a few minutes later asking her the same thing. She replied:

Sorry, guys. Can't. ☹ Family stuff.

She hated being stuck at home just because her new stepsister couldn't unpack her own stuff. A few more texts came in from dead people, but Anna ignored them all.

The room was still stacked with packed boxes. Anna took a good look around. Tabitha had been given her choice of several rooms and this was the one she'd picked. Anna could see why. Aside from having her own bathroom, Tabitha also had a queen-sized bed, a couch, and love seat. A mini-fridge sat near a bookshelf. Anna's mom had put up some shelves and had even bought her these cool acrylic nesting tables. Tabitha basically had her own apartment.

That night at dinner, Tabitha didn't say a word, no matter how many times Anna's mom asked questions or included her in a conversation. Tabitha would just shrug and look down at her dinner plate, pushing her food around with a fork. She had barely eaten anything when she excused herself to her room.

"Just give her a little time," Winston said after Tabitha left. He chuckled. "Once she gets comfortable, you won't be able to shut her up!"

After dinner, Anna texted Eden.

Tab doesn't seem bad. Just really quiet and sad.

That doesn't sound like her. At all.

Maybe she has changed?

I wouldn't count on it.

Maybe Eden had misjudged her. Tabitha had gone through a lot this last year, and if anyone could understand, it was Anna.

As Anna got ready for bed, she realized Tabitha probably was nervous about starting school in the morning. It didn't sound like she had left on good terms, and the students at Winchester Academy definitely judged outsiders. If Tabitha was anything like her, she probably wouldn't sleep tonight. She decided to run downstairs to Tabitha's room and tell her she knew what she was going through. And that she would help her any way she could.

Tabitha's bedroom door was open. Anna knocked, peeking in. The light in the adjoining bathroom was on. When she walked in, she found Tabitha washing her face in the sink.

"What are you doing in my room?" Tabitha pulled her dark red lips into a snarl, examining Anna behind her in the mirror.

Her attitude was anything but tiny.

"Uh . . . I just wanted to say good night. I've heard a lot about you, and—"

"Liar."

Anna blinked. "What?"

"I've heard nothing at all about you. Didn't even know Dad married again. So I'm pretty sure you didn't know a thing about me either."

"He didn't tell you he was getting married?"

Tabitha splashed her face with water. "Married?" She laughed. "He didn't even tell me he was dating. Or engaged."

Anna swallowed. "Well, it happened really fast. They were only engaged for like a second—"

"And then, as if that wasn't bad enough, I'm forced to move *here*." She pivoted toward Anna. "This place is like a haunted mansion right out of the movies."

"I felt like that too," Anna said, trying hard to be nice. "My mom wanted you to feel at home. She hung up those shelves and bought you new bedding at the same place she got mine. And—"

Tabitha snorted. "Oh, look, we have so much in common." She turned back to the mirror and pumped some pink facial gel into her palms and began slathering it over her face.

Anna took a deep breath. "Look, I just wanted to say good luck at school tomorrow."

Tabitha put her washcloth down. "Are you threatening me, Annabel?"

"What? No . . . I mean, it's tough to make friends there, and—"

"Really? Are you going to act like it's not your fault?"

Anna shook her head. "Like what's not my fault?"

Tabitha angrily splashed water on her face, patted it dry, and began applying moisturizer. "That you went broadcasting to the whole school that you live in Maddsen Manor and your mom married the undertaker. Because telling everyone your business really helps to make friends."

"How do you know what other people might or might not know?"

"You don't think I still have friends that keep me in the loop?" Tabitha chuckled. "Let's move this along, because I have to get up early. And this little meet-and-greet is really going to set the bags off under my eyes." She spit the words out like a bad taste.

"You'll recover," Anna threw back.

Tabitha glared at Anna in the mirror.

Great, Anna thought. *If looks could kill.* An icy chill penetrated her bones. Anna would probably be the one with bags under her eyes by morning, seeing as how she'd need to sleep with one eye open.

Or both.

"Ha! You are afraid," Tabitha said, more to herself than to Anna. "Maybe this won't be so bad after all."

"What are you talking about? And afraid of what? You?" Anna let out a big, fake laugh. "Especially not of you."

I've met lots of people scarier than you, Anna thought as images of Lucy and Harper came to mind.

And little did Tabitha know that one of them happened to be living in this very house.

CHAPTER 11

Harper

Harper was firm. "No way! I'm not crawling through some tunnel and wrinkling my outfit."

"You don't have to crawl." Eden smoothed out the wrinkles on the original blueprint of Maddsen Manor

that she had conjured up using a locator spell. It had been folded in one of the heavy books on the top shelf in the library.

"I think your clothes should be the least of your problems," Anna added.

Harper frowned. She'd decided she did not like Anna. At all. "I don't have money like I did in my former life. I can't exactly buy new clothes."

"Your former life was like a week ago," Eden pointed out. "Not that much has changed."

"I'm not talking about a week ago." Harper sighed. "Forget it. So where's this secret tunnel?"

Eden pointed to the blueprint. "It looks like the tunnel starts in one of the second-floor rooms."

The three of them pounded down the staircase to the floor below.

"Which room?" Anna was out of breath. *And way out of shape,* Harper thought snidely.

They followed Eden, stopping at the last door in the hallway.

"This room is huge. How are we going to find something in here that's supposed to be hidden?" Harper complained when they walked inside.

Eden held up the paper and waved it in front of Harper. "Hello. Why do you think I have the floor plan?"

"Okay then, genius," Harper said, putting her hands on her hips. Her body had finally started to feel real again, and she squeezed her hip bones extra hard. "Where is it?"

Eden rolled her eyes. "That wall." She pointed to the wall on the left. Set into the middle of it was a fireplace, flanked by a bookcase on one side and a closet on the other.

"So it's either the bookcase, which is so cliché, or we're going to Narnia," Harper said.

"Or it could be in the fireplace," Anna said.

"Doubt it. That would be pretty stupid to build a fire in the same place you want to escape through," Harper said. "I mean, come on."

"That would actually be smart," Anna said primly.

Harper was ready to throw Anna into a fire right about now.

Each girl started investigating, Eden pushing and pulling at boards and bricks, Harper knocking and rapping against the wall. Anna was stomping around the room like an elephant.

"Can you do that a little quieter? Like, not at all?" Harper suggested.

Anna ignored her. "There might be something on the floor. You never know."

"Got it!" Eden jumped up, waving the other girls over excitedly.

"The fireplace? Really?" Harper said.

"Told you," Anna said happily.

Eden pushed on the tiles that formed the back of the fireplace and a door inched open, creaking and groaning after being sealed so long.

Harper peered into an abyss of darkness. "How am I supposed to see in there?"

"Chill." Eden pulled out her phone and turned on its flashlight.

In front of them were short, narrow concrete steps that spiraled down. The light didn't reach the bottom, so the staircase looked never ending.

"All right, who's going first?" Harper asked.

Eden and Anna looked at Harper.

"Of course." Harper planted her hands on her hips. "It's always the undead girl. Never the witch or ghost whisperer."

• • •

The passage led to a door at the very back of Maddsen Manor, facing the cemetery. If you didn't know the door was there, you'd never see it from the outside. It was covered by an overgrowth of shrubs and weeds.

It had taken Harper about five minutes to make it through the cobweb-filled passageway. She ran her fingers through her hair and brushed off her clothes to make sure no bugs were on her. She'd heard a story on the news once about a spider that had crawled into a woman's ear and spun a web inside her ear canal. The woman thought she was hearing things—but what she was hearing was an actual spider.

Harper hated spiders. And worms. And anything that lived in the dirt.

Harper glanced over at the cemetery. A wave of fear and gratitude passed over her. At least she wasn't there. She had gotten another chance at life.

She gazed back at creepy, decrepit Mad Manor, her eyes drawn inexplicably upward.

Someone was watching her from a second-story window.

. . .

Later that night, Lucy appeared in Harper's new room as she was writing in her latest journal. She'd found a stack of dusty, empty notebooks on a bedroom shelf. Bored, she'd picked one up. She'd always kept a diary. Her new life would be no different.

This is the diary of Harper Sweety

Dear Diary,
You won't believe the day I've had.

"Ooh, whatcha writing about?" Lucy asked, peeking over her shoulder.

"Leave me alone." Harper kept writing.

"Is that any way for you to talk to someone who

gave you your life back?" Lucy flickered out and reappeared next to Harper, sitting on the edge of her desk.

Harper sighed, setting her pencil down, and turned in her chair to face Lucy. "Let me guess." Harper crossed her arms. "You're here to collect on your favor."

"And smart!" Lucy beamed. "I like that."

Harper closed her diary. "Just tell me what you want."

Lucy crossed her legs, bouncing the right leg on top. "I want you to become friends with Tabitha."

"Anna's sister?"

"*Step*sister," Lucy corrected.

"Why do you want me to be friends with her?" Harper asked warily.

But Lucy brushed her off. "You don't need to worry about the reasons. Just do like I ask. Become her best friend. Get her to trust you."

"And then what?"

Lucy's eyes glinted. "I'll tell you later, when the time comes."

Harper shrugged. "Whatever." She swiveled back around and opened up the diary.

Dead people are so weird.

Behind her, Lucy smiled as she slowly vanished.

CHAPTER 12

ANNA

It shouldn't have been a surprise that Tabitha became the center of attention at the Academy. But it wasn't like the attention Anna had received when she was the new girl. Maybe it was because Tabitha had gone to school there before. But what really surprised Anna

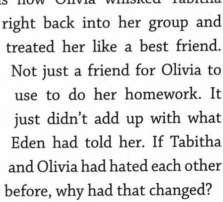

was how Olivia whisked Tabitha right back into her group and treated her like a best friend. Not just a friend for Olivia to use to do her homework. It just didn't add up with what Eden had told her. If Tabitha and Olivia had hated each other before, why had that changed?

"Olivia's trying to get back at me," Eden whispered as they walked down the hallway to their next class.

"Get back at you for what?" Anna asked. "For having your own friends and not letting her boss you around anymore? Hardly sounds like something she needs to get revenge for."

Eden slung her tote bag over her shoulder. "Hate to play the old evil-twin/good-twin card, but it's true. Trying to make my life miserable only makes her little black heart beat with pleasure. She's not a good person. Look at the way she treated you."

How could Anna forget? When Anna had first started school at Winchester Academy, Olivia had conned her into doing all her homework, as well as that of her mean-girl clique. When Olivia said jump, Anna did. Now she couldn't believe how gullible she had been. No, not even gullible. Desperate for friends. Desperate to fit in. But she had already found a great friend in Millie. She shouldn't have tried so hard.

Even if Millie was a ghost.

And her great-aunt.

"I miss Millie." Anna looked sadly at Eden. "Is there a way we can call her back? Could you cast a spell or something?"

Eden shook her head. "Sorry. But she'll come back. When the time is right." Eden winked, flinging her golden-blond strands over her shoulder. She had changed her hair color from platinum blond in an attempt to not be mistaken for Olivia.

Anna wished she had even an ounce of Eden's confidence. But unlike hair color, it seemed like something you had to be born with.

. . .

After lunch, Eden grabbed Anna's arm as they were walking down the hallway. "Look who's with them!" she whisper-yelled.

"Olivia, Tabitha, and . . . Harper?" Anna glanced at Eden. "What's going on?"

Eden shrugged, not taking her eyes off the group.

It was always Olivia and her clones that walked the halls. But Olivia's other friends were nowhere to be seen. Harper was wearing Anna's jeans and the new top her mom had let her buy at Forever 21.

Anna could feel steam pouring out her ears. How dare Harper raid her closet?

The two groups glared at each other in an uncomfortable silence as they passed each other. Anna half expected a musical gang fight to break out.

Hating confrontation to the fullest, Anna decided not to even mention the fact that Harper was wearing her clothes. Instead, she looped her arm through Eden's, pulling her around the wicked trio, in time to see Olivia's eyes smolder with anger.

There had to be more to Olivia's nasty attitude than she knew, Anna decided. All her oozing hatred had to come from somewhere, and Anna wasn't buying the whole evil-twin thing. People weren't born evil. Something made Olivia that way. If only Anna could figure out what it was.

Anna should've known she'd be running into one of them again later that day. Harper pretended not to see Anna in the hallway between classes, and bumped right into her. Hard. Anna's books went sailing out of her arms and scattered, littering the hallway. She felt like the scene was pulled right out of a teen movie.

Eden bent down to help as Anna looked over her shoulder. "Excuse you!" she yelled. Harper acted like she didn't hear her as she popped her shoulder back into its socket, not even flinching in pain.

"What the—" Anna stared after her.

"Hey, you dropped something!" some guy yelled as he stepped over the mess, chuckling.

"Yeah, thanks for helping, jerk." Anna's day was definitely not going as planned. Neither was her life.

CHAPTER 13

ANNA

Later that night, Anna's mom agreed to let Anna hang out at the clubhouse. She didn't have much homework, since it was a Friday. And her mom was so worn out from work that she didn't even bother grilling her on the who-what-when-where-and-why's. Although Winston decided to intervene.

"Take Tabitha with you. It would be good for her to make friends and start fitting in."

Anna wanted to tell him no, and that Tabitha was definitely fitting in wickedly well all on her own, but she bit her tongue. There was no point in arguing, since she already knew Tabitha wouldn't go anywhere with her.

Winston called Tabitha downstairs. "Anna's going out with some friends and wants you to join her," he said. "How about it, honey?"

Anna raised an eyebrow.

"I'd love to. Thank you for thinking of me, Anna," Tabitha said sweetly.

"What?" Anna stared at Tabitha in disbelief.

"I knew you girls would get along wonderfully!" Mom clapped her hands together. "Didn't I tell you, Winston?" She gazed at him with a lovey-dovey look that made Anna want to gag.

"Yes, you did." He smiled, looking from his daughter to Anna, although the smile didn't quite reach his eyes.

Anna was pretty sure he could see right through Tabitha's little act. Maybe he would put an end to this and call her out. Force her to stay home. Or better yet, send her packing back to her mother in Manhattan. Anna put on her coat and sneakers and slid her phone into her back pocket. Hopefully, the dead would leave her alone tonight. She hadn't had any messages today on her iPad. Maybe that was a good sign.

Outside, a car honked.

"That must be Eden's dad," Anna said. "He's giving us a ride there. I think we'll probably walk home, though."

"Call us if you need a ride," her mom said. "Otherwise, home by eleven!"

"Okay, you girls have fun!" Winston practically pushed them out the door.

Eden was sitting in the passenger seat of her dad's car, and when she saw Tabitha, she gave Anna a sideways glance.

"I'll tell you later," Anna mumbled, sliding into the backseat after Tabitha.

Tabitha avoided eye contact and stared out her window.

"So, change of plans," Eden said, holding up her phone. "Everyone is hanging out at Spencer's house instead."

Anna got along well with Spencer. They'd totally bonded after realizing Lucy was haunting both of them. But Anna hadn't talked to him much since Johnny's accident. He had seemed kind of distant. Maybe he thought the ghost thing was contagious and didn't want to take chances hanging around her again.

This was the first time Anna had been to Spencer's, but she knew he lived in one of the largest homes in the village, even larger than the Ashburys', within a gated community.

Mr. Ashbury gave his name to security and the guard punched in a code. The wooden arm in front of the car lifted to let them through.

Access granted.

They drove down a winding lane flanked with pines. The sprawling homes they passed were each more extravagant than the next. The car finally pulled into a circular driveway that sat in front of a huge, modern-looking glass-walled edifice that was lit up like a diamond. A giant chandelier sparkled from the second-story window. Water glistened as it cascaded from the enormous three-tiered fountain that was the centerpiece to the driveway.

And an unearthly glow emanated from twin statues that flanked the entranceway, giving Anna a creeped-out feeling.

She was hypnotized by the grandeur of the home. It was like the Manor times five. And it looked brand new, not gaudy and old and reeking of death.

Once Mr. Ashbury had pulled away, Eden led them in through the front door without even knocking. To say it was noisy was an understatement. Anna's chest picked up the bass from a song she didn't recognize as an army of shadows laughed and danced to the beat.

Eden leaned into Anna. "Arfu mmph glickwr," she said.

"What?" Anna shouted. "I can't understand a word

you're saying." The music was so loud she thought her eardrums were going to blow out.

Tabitha suddenly leaped across the room. "Spencer!" There he was, sporting his trademark large black glasses and wearing a flannel shirt, his hair floppy. Tabitha flung her arms around him. Anna's stomach gave a tight pinch.

He made eye contact with Anna over Tabitha's shoulder and gave her a wink.

"How did that happen?" Eden shouted over the music.

Anna shrugged. "Didn't know they were so close."

"Look who decided to join the party." Olivia crept up, looking right at Anna as she spoke.

Tabitha crossed over the invisible line to enemy territory and stood beside Olivia.

Without a word, Eden pulled Anna away and guided her across the room and through a set of double doors that led to the backyard. It was really cold out. As cold as a mausoleum must be, Anna thought, shivering.

She tried to blink away scary thoughts. Why did her mind always have to be cluttered with death?

. . .

An hour later, Spencer's party was still going strong. Aside from bumping into Olivia when they'd first arrived, Anna hadn't seen her since. Which normally would've been a good thing, except Anna couldn't leave without Tabitha.

"Did you call her?" Eden asked.

"Yeah, and texted. She's either ignoring me or her phone is dead."

"Probably the first option."

"Yeah." Anna had decided to walk home, and it was already 10:45 p.m., which didn't give them much time.

"Hey, I found her." Eden pointed to the room across the hall.

Anna heard Tabitha's voice as she got closer and stopped in mid-step. "Is that Johnny she's talking to?"

"Kind of sounds like it."

Sure enough, Tabitha was with Johnny, doing her sickly-sweet fake voice and laughing at every word he said. Anna and Eden hovered outside the doorway, making sure to keep out of sight.

"Anna really said that?" Johnny said.

Anna's ears perked up at the mention of her name. She pulled Eden closer to listen.

"Yep," Tabitha said. "Isn't she just horrible? She even said she would sabotage me at school to make sure I didn't have a single friend."

"Well, you have me," Johnny said, and Anna didn't need to see him to know that he was probably smiling down at her.

Anna leaned back in the hall, filled with disbelief. How was it that nobody could see past Tabitha's fakeness? "I want to go now." Her knees trembled as she tried to steady herself against the wall.

"What about *her*?"

"Forget her. She can find her own way home."

CHAPTER 14

ANNA

It was late in the afternoon the next day when Anna finally rolled out of bed. She had two missed calls on her phone and several texts. One was sent from Tabitha's phone, but it was from Harper. And it had been sent only a few minutes ago.

> Guess who my new bestie is? That's right. Your stepsister. And you're in huge trouble. Just thought you should know ☺

"What?" Anna gasped. When had that happened? This was going to be really, really bad. Her stepsister and her ungrateful undead/dead "friend" were now besties? What had Harper told Tabitha?

Anna had crept in last night and gone straight to bed. She had no idea when—or how—Tabitha got home. And frankly she didn't care. But still, her stomach was a pit of snakes and she got chills just thinking about dealing with the wrath of her mom.

Anna found her mom in the kitchen. Which meant Winston had to be near.

"How could you leave your stepsister like that? She didn't get home until one a.m.! We were worried sick!" Her mom went on and on about how awful Anna was, and how poor Tabitha had the worst night in the world.

"So what's the damage?" Anna wanted to get straight to the point. "Am I grounded a week? Two weeks?"

Her mom's eyes widened as she glanced behind her. "I was able to get your punishment lessened to a week," she said in a guilty whisper.

"Why are you whispering?" Anna asked. "And what do you mean you were able to get it lessened?"

"Winston was saying a month. But I thought that was a little much."

"Winston? Why is he deciding how long I'm punished for? *You're* my mom."

"Yes, but he's your stepdad now," her mom said.

"Exactly. *Step*dad. Not my *real* dad." Anna said the last part louder than necessary.

Anna's mom started unloading the dishwasher. "Spare the attitude. We're a family now. A *real* family."

"Because what, we were a fake family before, when it was just me and you?" Anna said, feeling tears welling up in her eyes. She couldn't help it. She hated Winston.

"Anna." Her mom's eyes softened with regret. "I didn't mean it like that."

"That's it," Winston barked, coming from behind Anna. "You don't talk to your mother like that."

Anna looked at her mom, who remained silent. Was she really backing him up on everything?

"Whatever." Anna didn't bother hanging around. Instead, she sped up the staircase.

Tabitha and Harper were sitting on the top step of the second flight of stairs.

"Yeah," Tabitha said in a mocking tone. "You really shouldn't talk to your mother like that."

"Just shut up," Anna said, pushing past them. "I thought you were 'out.'" She made air quotes when she said "out." She was dying to know what Tabitha knew about Harper and vice versa, but she didn't want to give them the satisfaction of asking them.

"Oops," Harper said. "I guess you never know where we'll be." She cracked her knuckles, and for a split second it looked as if one of her fingers bent abnormally sideways.

"There's no way we were going to miss this show," Tabitha said, gloating. "Especially after I told my dad how you ditched me and left me all alone to wander the woods. In the dark. Late at night."

"Anything could've happened to her," Harper said sympathetically.

. . .

As soon as Anna got to her room, she locked and bolted the door. Then she called up Eden and told her everything.

"She said she had to walk home?" Eden laughed. "Spencer's dad drove Tabitha and Harper home soon after you left."

"Unbelievable!" Anna felt like punching a wall. "My mom said they didn't get home till one a.m. She said Tabitha's sweater was ripped and her face was streaked with dirt and tears, her elbows skinned. She claimed to have rolled out of the way of an oncoming speeding car."

"Yeah, that she threw herself in front of. Wow. Your mom got played."

"She even told Harper what a great friend she was for sticking by her and staying the night to make sure everything was okay." Anna threw her arms in the air. "How is she able to just move in and ruin my life?"

"Well, you know what you gotta do, right?"

Anna found herself nodding. "Play the game better than her." She was ready to do whatever it took to send Tabitha running all the way back to her mom's. And then she was going to have to get rid of Harper. For good.

But to play, they were going to need some help.

Help from the other side.

Although there was one problem.

Spirits contacted Anna easily. But this time, she was the one who was going to have to do the contacting.

CHAPTER 15

Monday couldn't come fast enough. Anna spent the morning trying to pay attention to her teachers—but all she could think about were her three problems.

Tabitha
Harper
Winston

During science class, her lab partner, Archer, kept glancing over at her. Anna pretended not to notice and kept her head down, acting as if she were writing notes. She remembered Archer from the Ashbury twins' big party at the start of the year. He had thick blond hair, wore preppy clothes, and generally looked nervous. And she'd seen him with Olivia sometimes. She didn't really know him, though. He didn't talk very much.

After the hundredth time she caught him staring, Anna gave up and sat back. "What?"

Archer looked around and then leaned toward her. His elbow rammed Anna's off the table. "Tabitha's your sister?"

Anna crossed her arms over her chest. "Step."

Archer nodded. "Is it true that her dad is the mortician?"

"Maybe you should ask her." Anna didn't want to be accused of "broadcasting her business" or anything.

"Oh." Archer's eyes kept darting around. "So is she nicer at home than she is at school?"

"What?"

"Well, she seems so . . . cold. You know, at school. Is she always like that?"

"You mean like Olivia?"

Archer's jaw dropped and Anna couldn't bite back a smile. "You can go ahead and tell her I said that."

"Tell Olivia? Why would I do that?"

"Um . . . because you're friends with her." Anna wasn't afraid of Olivia. Not anymore. Anna had battled against ghosts and lots of unpleasant deadly things. Olivia was just a regular girl who thrived on power. As long as everyone gave it to her, nothing would change. But Anna wasn't contributing to it.

Archer rolled his eyes. "You've got that wrong. I'm not friends with her. Not since the *accident*." He whispered the last part, and Anna knew he was talking about Lucy's accident.

"What's that have to do with you?" Anna asked, frowning.

"Lucy Edwards was my cousin."

Anna's mouth quirked up. "You're related to Lucy?"

"Yeah. We weren't close, but still, she's family. How can I be friends with someone who tried to hurt her?"

"Hurt her?" Anna asked.

"Well, yeah. You saw how Olivia made fun of her every chance she got."

"Right." Anna nodded absentmindedly. Except Archer had still seemed like friends with Olivia the night of the party. Before Lucy's accident. And why had he stood by watching stuff happen to Lucy if he was so against it?

"So why exactly did Olivia push Johnny that night?" he asked. "I could never figure that out."

Almost everybody thought that Olivia was the one who'd caused Johnny's accident. Anna was the only one who knew the truth. "Did someone put you up to asking me? Like Olivia?"

He groaned. "Like I told you, we aren't friends. But you seem cool, Anna. I wish we could be friends."

"Friends are overrated." Anna repeated the line Millie had used.

"Not if you've got good ones."

"And you're saying you're going to be a good one?" Anna asked. She definitely needed all the living friends she could get . . . but she had to make sure she could trust them first.

"Better than most of the people in this school."

Anna nodded. This whole conversation was a little strange. Archer had to have a motive.

The bell rang and Anna scooted her chair back. "Time to go." She needed a good nap. Or coma.

Archer followed Anna as she shouldered her way out the door and to her locker. "I mean it, Anna. I'm not a bad guy. You can trust me."

"Uh-huh. Sure." She would say anything to have Archer quit talking. Finally he got the hint and walked away.

But the misery continued.

Anna groaned inwardly as she ran into her favorite person ever.

"Annabel." Olivia tilted her chin up and her blue eyes flashed as she flipped her platinum-blond hair over her shoulder.

"Olivia." Anna stepped to the left to move past her. Olivia blocked her.

"What do you want?" Anna asked.

"Johnny is mine."

Anna laughed. "Good for you." She moved to the right but Olivia blocked her again.

Olivia narrowed her eyes. "Johnny likes me too."

"And?"

"So back off."

"I can be friends with anyone I want."

Olivia moved closer and said quietly, "Well, he wants nothing to do with you."

"I'm surprised he wants anything to do with *you*." Anna could feel her face heating up.

"Oh? And why is that?" Olivia gave a fake smile.

"Because everyone knows you were the one who hurt him! Glass table ring a bell?" Anna clamped her mouth closed, wishing she could suck the words back in. Someone gasped. Someone else laughed. A few people moved closer.

Olivia's smug smile slipped. She pulled at her short, barely there skirt and readjusted her hold on her books. Students had stopped to watch, hoping for a catfight. Anna could hear whispers of people walking past. She knew this would soon be all over school, if it wasn't already.

"Oh yeah?"

"Is that the best you can come up with?" Anna said. "It. Wasn't. Me."

Anna caught sight of Archer on the sidelines. He pointed to the corner. When Anna looked over, she saw Johnny leaning against the wall with some of his football buddies. He brushed some of his dark hair out of his eyes and rubbed his temples.

Tabitha pushed through the crowd and sidled next to Olivia. "What's going on, Liv?"

"You sister here just accused me of something." Olivia's eyes drilled into Anna. "And I'm done. I'm going to once and for all prove it wasn't me!"

"You can't prove something if it isn't true," Anna blurted out. What was wrong with her? It was like she didn't have control over her words. Almost like—

Anna scanned the crowd and caught sight of Eden. Her witchy friend winked when they made eye contact.

Eden! Anna silently screamed. *I'm so going to get you for this!*

People had their phones out. Anna was pretty sure somebody had to be filming this. She pushed through her gaping classmates.

Archer walked over. "Did you see how Johnny was watching you? I think he was really concerned."

Anna shook her head. He was confused, not concerned. Big difference.

"He likes you. You guys would be perfect together. I can tell."

Anna snorted. "How?"

"What?"

"How can you tell? You know nothing about me."

"Well . . . okay. But I'm being honest here—there's something special about you now. Although you weren't all that fabulous when you first started here."

"It hasn't even been a year."

"But still. I knew who you were. Well, everyone did. That happens when you're new. You stick out like a sore thumb." Archer paused. "Sorry, no offense."

"None taken." Anna sighed.

"But then something changed in you over just the last few months. I have no idea what, but it's like you don't care anymore about all the popularity stuff." Archer shrugged. "I know it sounds stupid, but there's something about you. Like you're a mystery or something. Then, just now, what you did, that took guts."

Anna cringed. It took a spell, not guts. "Well, everyone shouldn't be so afraid of the popular crowd."

"It's easy for someone like you to say that," Archer said, wiggling his blond eyebrows.

Anna pulled him over to the side, by the lockers. "What are you talking about?"

"*I know,*" he whispered.

"Know what?" Anna's blood froze.

Archer looked around. Then he lowered his voice. "I know your secret. But it's okay. I'm not going to say a word."

Anna frowned. How did Archer know anything? She had barely spoken two words to him before today.

"Look, Anna. Just know you're awesome. Olivia tried to decimate you and you got away from her. And made her look stupid too. No one does that."

"Thanks," Anna said. And she meant it. She wasn't sure that Archer knew her real secret—that she was a Guided, a bridge to the other side. But she could always use a friend in this school.

Especially one who was alive.

CHAPTER 16

ANNA

Anna felt better after calling Eden.

"I doubt he knows anything. Even if he did, nobody would ever believe him," Eden said.

"Yeah. You're right," Anna said. "I barely believe it myself."

Anna hadn't stopped thinking about contacting a spirit. And the spirit she wanted to contact was that of her estranged great-uncle, Maxwell Maddsen. If any spirit was going to help her, one that was related to her was her best shot. As much as she wanted to see Millie again, Anna knew there were reasons why she hadn't appeared despite Anna wishing she would.

She and Eden had decided to try contacting Maxwell through a séance. Anna didn't know the first thing about how to do one, though, so she went searching online at the Academy's library and then at the town's public library. She found nothing on the subject.

There really should be a book out there called *Séances for Dummies*, Anna thought as she plunked down in the oversized leather chair in the Manor's own library. Even if she figured out how to do it, there was no guarantee it would actually work.

We really could use your help, Uncle Max.

Anna sucked in a deep breath, taking in the faint scent of cigars. She was pretty sure Maxwell had had a thing for cigars when he was alive. And ships. Her eyes roamed around the room's nautical-themed decor, from the sails that covered one wall to the rope along the top of the bookshelf.

Not so long ago she thought she'd never go near this room again. After a recently departed Lucy had shown herself here and thrown hardcover books at her—those books were heavy!—Anna had been afraid of a repeat. But once she realized Lucy could get to her from anywhere, she was more afraid of the actual ghost than any room. Which made her think . . . would Lucy try visiting her again when she least expected it?

Anna's eyes darted quickly around the room. She didn't want to get caught in a hailstorm of books again. But she did want to confront Lucy.

Anna's gaze landed on a book that rested on the upper bookshelves. It stuck out a little further than the others. She pushed the library ladder in front of the shelves and climbed up. Most of the books on the shelves were dusty, with wrinkled bindings, but this book looked shiny and new.

Séances for the Beginner.

This was definitely a sign.

"Thanks," she whispered to the unknown spirit that had helped her.

Anna took the book down and began to read. After an hour, her head felt as if it would burst from everything she'd tried to cram in there.

She hadn't realized there were so many written rules for everything.

AS YOU PREPARE FOR A SÉANCE . . .

Rule #1: Keep an open mind
Rule #2: Three or more people is best.

Rule #3: Never conduct a séance by yourself, unless you want to go insane.

Rule #4: Set up a spirit-friendly environment.

Rule #5: Spirits come out at night, so any ritual should be performed in the evening for best results.

Anna laughed. Who wrote these rules? She had been contacted day and night by spirits when her mind had been closed, locked, and sealed. Although she had to maybe agree with the insane part.

Anna blew the hair out of her eyes as she began skimming through the second half of the book, which was full of useful information. Periodically she paused and took a picture with her phone of anything that seemed particularly relevant.

WHAT YOU NEED TO COMPLETE A SÉANCE:

1. A Table—round or oval.

Anna giggled. Apparently ghosts were afraid of corners.

2. A White Tablecloth/Sheet/Paper: The color white will help attract the "good" spirits

and prevent them from wanting to sleep
over.

Darn, thought Anna, *I really wanted a ghost slumber
party too.*

3. Lots and Lots of Unscented Candles
    (minimum of three): Please try to use white
    and purple candles for spirituality. These are
    to be placed in the center of the table.
4. An Assortment of Scented Candles: to be
    placed around the room.
    Cinnamon to provide warmth and energy.
    Frankincense to aid in meditation.
    Sandalwood to help you stay focused.
5. Meditation Music: mild and soothing,
    to help you relax and to set the mood.
    IMPORTANT NOTE: Turn it off before
    actually performing séance!
6. A Voice Recorder: so that you can listen to
    the session later.
7. A Medium: one person to conduct the
    séance. Someone in tune with their sixth
    sense.

Anna stopped at the eighth item:

8. A Recently Deceased Spirit: Try not to summon a spirit who's been dead for a super long time. They usually don't want to be bothered and may get angry over this.

Wasn't that the whole point of this? Not the angry part but the bothering part?

9. A Charging Session for the Candles: Everyone should take turns holding each candle and visualizing the symbolic power coming from it. When you look at the white candle, imagine strands of peaceful smoke curling up. Each candle should be passed and held by each person before placing it in the center of the table.

All I ever needed was a phone, Anna thought, sighing. *And it didn't even need to be charged.*

CHAPTER 17
ANNA

Eden laughed as her eyes skimmed over Anna's séance notes. "Is this for real?"

"According to the book I read," Anna said. "Crazy, right?"

"That's putting it mildly."

"And we only have two people," Anna pointed out. "Not three."

"Do you really think we need three? None of the other stuff makes sense, so why would that?"

"I know, but . . . I don't think we should take a chance," Anna said. What if there was a little bit of truth to it? "Who will be our third?"

"What about your new lab friend?" Eden asked.

"Archer?" Anna wasn't sure about that. "What

would I say to him? 'Hey, you want to help me contact my dead uncle because I need help getting rid of my evil stepsister and her zombie friend'?"

"No!" Eden snorted. "I can do a 'before' spell that makes him completely open-minded to the idea and an 'after' spell so he'll forget."

Anna felt a little guilty that they were about to put a spell on an innocent victim. But they didn't have choice.

"Let's do it."

• • •

Convincing Archer wasn't as hard as Anna thought it would be. Eden used the lowest dose of the spell on him the next day at school, and even with that, he was more than willing to be an active participant. He'd arrived at Anna's house at eight p.m. Anna's mom and Winston had gone to a movie.

"Okay, guys." He clapped. "Let's get our ghost on!" He threw his hands in the air and let out a whoop.

Eden and Anna turned to look at Archer.

"Did . . . you just try to raise the roof?" Eden asked.

Archer placed his hands in his lap and smoothed out the wrinkles from his canvas pants. "Sorry. I'll control myself."

They sat on Anna's bed, with the door closed, and

the only light came from the moon shining through the slits in the blinds.

"Okay, so it says that in order to summon a spirit," Anna said, flipping to the next page in the book, "we have to join hands and close our eyes."

They moved to the floor and sat cross-legged on the purple rug. They held hands and closed their eyes while Anna read the next steps.

"Breathe slowly, in and out. Keep your mind blank. You'll want to be calm, comfy, and alert."

"That's a lot to think about when you're supposed to keep your mind blank," Archer whispered.

"Just try," Eden whispered back out of the side of her mouth.

"Now," Anna continued, "we need to chant this next part together and repeat it until we get a response. 'Our beloved Maxwell Maddsen, we ask that you commune with us and move among us.'"

Anna lifted her head from the book and closed her eyes as all three of them repeated together, "Our beloved Maxwell Maddsen, we ask that you commune with us and move among us."

Nothing.

Archer coughed as they continued to chant.

"Our beloved Maxwell Maddsen, we ask that you commune with us and move among us."

Nothing.

"Concentrate," Anna whispered.

"Our beloved Maxwell Maddsen, we ask that you commune with us and move among us."

"Please," added Archer.

Anna peeked at Archer. His face was bunched up and his eyelids were wrinkled from being closed so tightly. He was almost concentrating *too much*.

They repeated the chant several more times, sometimes stumbling on their words and getting out of sync.

A door slammed.

"Oh my God!" Archer jumped, eyes as round as saucers. "It's a sign. What do we do now?"

"Well, we don't freak out. That was just one of the doors closing downstairs below us. It was only a sign that Tabitha is home."

"But it could've been something more. I mean, how can you be so sure?"

Eden and Anna exchanged looks.

"Well," Anna said, "it says once we receive a sign, we ask him to knock once if this is him, or two if not. But since you broke the circle, we'll have to start all over again. From the beginning."

Eden let out a frustrated sigh.

"Sorry," Archer muttered as he sat back down.

They repeated the chant only three times before asking for a knock.

"Knock once if you are here, Maxwell. Knock twice if this is someone else."

Silence.

"Knock once if you are here—"

Their voices were cut off by a sound coming from outside the bedroom door. They all turned toward it.

Knock.

Knock.

Knock.

The knocking was slow and deliberate at first, with a pause between each rap. Then it became repetitious and faster.

Knock, knock, knock.

Knock, knock, knock.

"So what do three knocks mean?" Archer's voice shook.

"If it's a bad spirit, we need to quickly tell it to go in peace, then blow out the candles, turn on the lights, and run!" Eden whispered.

The three jumped, blowing out the candles and turning on the lights. When they started to run toward the door, Eden stopped them. "Shhhhh!" She froze mid-movement and held her finger up. "Listen."

Anna strained her ears, and only then did she hear the noise. Barely. She quickly tiptoed to the door, with Archer right behind her doing the same. Anna turned the knob. She threw the door open and jumped back, bumping into Archer. "Ow! Sorry!"

Tabitha and Harper were crouched down by the door in a fit of giggles. They laughed even harder when they saw Anna's face.

"Make it stop! My stomach hurts!" Tabitha had tears running down her face.

"That . . . was . . . great!" Harper couldn't talk without gasping for air. "Spirits!"

"Ghosts!"

"So . . . ridiculous! Who really . . . believes in . . . that stuff?"

Eden stepped around the two. "C'mon, you guys. We're outta here." Anna and Archer followed without hesitation.

"Hey, Ghost Ghouls, can I join your club?" Tabitha shouted.

CHAPTER 18

Harper

"That was great!" Tabitha stood up and leaned against Anna's doorway.

"Yeah, who knew they believed in stuff like that?" Harper said, laughing.

"So lame."

"Totally."

Harper jumped as the front door slammed downstairs.

"Do I have any black under my eyes?" Tabitha swiped a finger under each eye, smudging her black liner even more.

"You look like—"

A loud thump from inside Anna's room made Tabitha jump. All the laughter died on their lips as they cautiously peeked inside the room. Everything looked in place. Except a large book lying on the ground.

"Maybe it fell?" Harper said nervously.

"From where? It's in the middle of the room."

Harper shrugged.

In slow motion, each candle in the room began flickering—first a spark, then a flame—until slowly, one by one, they were all lit. The flames danced higher and higher, casting eerie shadows along the wall.

Tabitha's mouth fell open. "Did you see that?"

"Uh-huh," Harper whispered. She herself had been a ghost for all of two seconds, and she was still creeped out by them.

Suddenly the door slammed shut in their faces, catching the tip of Harper's finger. Tabitha took off running down the stairs while Harper stared at her detached finger wiggling in the crack of the door.

She looked down at her hand with only four fingers now. There was no blood. No pain. But it looked like . . . well, what a hand with a recently severed finger should look like.

She pulled on the wiggling finger but it wouldn't budge. Harper slowly opened the door, half expecting it to be locked. It opened easily and her finger fell with a thud to the ground.

She picked it up, amazed at how it still seemed to

have a life of its own while it moved wormlike in her palm.

Maybe it was out of instinct, or just came from watching too many late-night horror movies, but Harper placed the finger back onto her knuckle, and it locked there like a perfect puzzle piece.

She moved her finger and it worked just fine, although there was a line around where it had been reconnected. She stepped back from the door as if it would slam closed at any moment. From a distance, she scanned the inside of the room to see if she could identify the reason for all the weird stuff that had just happened. She pushed the door open more, quickly pulling back her hand.

The room was empty. But that book . . . the one that had been in the middle of the room before . . . it was gone. Her eyes searched the room until she spotted it on the purple nightstand by Anna's bed.

"Freakin' ghosts," she muttered. "They've overrun this house like termites or something. . . ." She trailed off as she spotted something silvery sparkling next to the mysterious moving book. With a cramp slowly tightening in her leg, she shuffled over to the nightstand. A ring was there.

She slid the shiny ring over her newly attached finger.

"Perfect." She admired her hand from afar and was pleased that the band concealed the line. And it fit perfectly, like it was meant for her.

"Harper!" Tabitha yelled from downstairs. "Where'd you go?"

"Coming!" Harper yelled back. And with a smug smile, she turned around and started running down the stairs to Tabitha's room. She only made it halfway down before she tripped, twisting her ankle.

Snap.

She felt the bone pop as her foot detached and rolled down the steps, landing with a final thud.

"Oh, this is so not good," Harper muttered.

CHAPTER 19
ANNA

"We are never going to hear the end of this," Anna said to Eden and Archer. The three of them were sitting on the front steps of Maddsen Manor.

"End of what?" Archer asked.

Anna shot a look at Eden.

"Yeah, I already did it." Eden was careful not to mention the word "spell." Or "ghosts."

Anna waved her hand toward the house. "You know, Tabitha and Harper never leaving us alone."

"Oh. Right."

Anna was thankful Archer didn't keep digging.

"So now what?" Eden asked.

Someone's phone chimed with a new text. They all pulled out their phones to check.

"It's mine." Anna said. She clamped a hand over her mouth as she read the text.

"What is it?" Eden leaned over to read the message on her screen.

Millie: Guess who? I'm baaack!

"Who's Millie?" Archer asked.

"She's, um, my cousin," Anna said. Admitting it was her long-dead great-aunt would totally give away her secrets.

"That's fantastic!" Eden turned to Archer. "She lives out of state, so Anna hasn't seen her for a while."

"A while" was actually only three months, but it seemed like forever since Anna had said goodbye to her best friend.

Anna texted Millie.

Where are you?

Are you really friends with Eden now?

Don't be like that. She's the exact opposite of what you thought.

I don't trust her.

It's OK. She knows about you. And she's a witch.

So is Olivia.

No, a REAL spell-casting, anti-broom-riding
witch.

IDK about that.

You trust me, right?

Of course!

Then trust me on this. Come out, k?

After your other friend leaves.

K.

"Well, it's getting late. I think I'm gonna head to
bed." Anna stretched her arms above her head, forcing
a long, drawn-out yawn.

Eden caught on immediately. "Oh yeah, me too."

"Oh, okay. I guess we'll leave, then." Archer looked
disappointed. "Want a ride home, Eden?"

"I just texted my mom. But thanks."

A few minutes later Archer's older sister pulled up.
"See ya at school!" Archer said, waving, as he got into
the car.

The car was barely out of sight before Anna and
Eden jumped up and ran upstairs to her room. Anna

locked her bedroom door and this time turned on her iPad music to drown out their talking in case of any possible eavesdroppers.

The air in front Anna seemed to thicken. A light shimmer appeared. Then, suddenly, she was looking at Millie.

"Millie!" Anna hugged her, not even caring that the coldness chilled her to her bones. "I'm so happy you're here!" A sweet smell of vanilla swirled in the air. "What made you decide to come back?"

Millie blinked at her. "What, you mean you weren't summoning me earlier? Asking me to knock?"

Anna laughed. "You were there!"

Millie nodded. Her vibrant red curly hair fell in ringlets to her shoulders. "Yes. I don't know where you came up with those rules, but you won't catch any ghosts doing that."

Anna hugged her again. "Well, we got your attention, didn't we?"

"What's she saying? What's going on?" Eden was looking right through Millie, unable to see her.

Anna pointed. "She said—"

Millie cut Anna off. "Hold on. It will be easier than trying to repeat everything."

Anna watched as Millie's shape shimmered so slightly that if she weren't watching she would have missed it.

Eden let out a squeal. "I can see you!"

"How are you able to do that?" Anna asked.

"I can make myself visible to others if I want to," Millie explained. "It just takes a lot of concentration and strength."

"Wouldn't that have made things so much easier if Lucy had just appeared to Johnny?" Anna thought about how many problems that would've saved.

Millie shook her head. "It takes a long time to learn how to do these fancy tricks. I've had decades of practice." She beamed at Anna. "And it took an enormous amount of her energy just to appear as soon as she did too. It drains her strength so that she can't appear again for a while."

"So the chant we did summoned you instead of Maxwell?" Eden asked.

"No, sadly, that chant didn't do anything," Millie said. "I've been here a few days. I was just deciding when I should pop in. I had some fun with your stepsister and her friend, so I'm sure you'll hear them whine about that soon enough. I wanted you to know it was me before you started thinking you summoned an evil spirit or whatever."

"Fun?" Eden repeated. "What did you do to Tabitha and Harper?"

"I definitely scared the crazy out of Tabitha. She

ran crying down the stairs," Millie said. "But I don't know about Harper. She didn't seem too scared."

"Probably because she used to be a ghost," Anna said.

"For like a week," added Eden.

"Then she took back her body," Anna went on. She explained the whole story to Millie.

"So what's the plan?" Millie asked.

"Plan?" the girls echoed.

Millie nodded. "You aren't actually going to let her live in an undead body, right?"

"We didn't think we had a choice," Anna said.

"There's always a choice." Millie said, hovering a bit higher off the ground. "Because her body's not really alive, it's not so easy to reclaim it." She twirled one of her long red ringlets. "When Harper ran after Tabitha, she tripped. And . . . her foot fell off. She put it back on, but . . ."

Anna's and Eden's jaws dropped as they exchanged looks.

"Okay, that's bad," Anna said.

Millie floated over to her and patted her shoulder.

"You know, I'm not used to seeing you as an actual ghost," Anna said, thinking back to when she had first started at Winchester Academy and had met Millie. Millie had really helped her get through those first scary days at school. "Did it take a lot of energy to look like you were alive?"

"Like you wouldn't believe," Millie said. "But if you want something bad enough, you'll find a way to overcome any obstacle."

Anna nodded. "Well, I guess the first thing I want to do is confront Lucy. I need to find out exactly what she told Harper. There's more to the story. I know it. But Harper refuses to talk." She paused. "Hey, Eden," she said, her mind speeding forward. "Do you happen to know a spell for making people tell the truth?"

Eden scrunched up her mouth. "Yeah. But . . ."

"But?" Anna prompted.

"I overused it a teeny tiny bit on Olivia and the spell got blocked. But I'll have access to it again when I'm sixteen."

"Hardly any help to us now." Anna sighed. "And unless we can think of another way to try to contact my uncle Maxwell, I'm out of ideas."

She thought back to Harper and her foot. "We have a huge problem," she said grimly.

"Yeah," said Eden. "But what's the solution?"

CHAPTER 20

ANNA

"C'mon, Lucy! Show yourself."

Nothing. Not even so much as a shimmer of air. Or the lingering scent of lemons that usually appeared whenever Lucy was near. Since talking with Millie and Eden last night, Anna was ready to kick some ghost butt.

"I know what you did. Stop being a scaredy-cat—er, ghost— and come out."

Anna threw her hands down. Why was she even

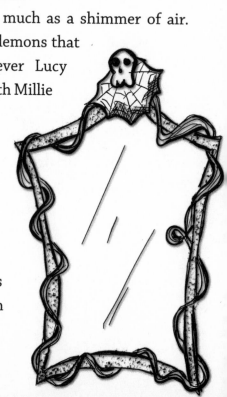

bothering? Lucy was probably hiding out somewhere far away where she wasn't likely to even hear Anna. Well, if that's how it worked. Maybe ghosts had supersonic hearing or something. Anything was possible.

Anna's phone pinged with a text.

"Aha! I knew you could hear me!" But Anna frowned as she looked at the screen.

I need help. Please.

The texter definitely wasn't Lucy. The word "please" wasn't even in her vocab. At least this anonymous spirit had manners.

Anna quickly typed a response:

What kind of help?

She felt like she was working on a ghost crisis hotline. She had thought, not that long ago, that the spirits simply passed around her number. But that wasn't the case at all.

I can't find my body.

What's your name? Alive or unsure? When did you first notice this problem?

> Mary. Not alive. Noticed this problem when my
> body left without me.

A knock sounded on Anna's bedroom door. "Yeah, come in," she answered without looking up, while texting back:

> Where did you lose your body?

"Did you mess with my room?" Tabitha stood in the doorway with a scowl.

Anna briefly looked up from the screen and rolled her eyes. "Why would I mess with your room?"

"Maybe you were snooping again."

"I wasn't snooping. I told you, I was looking for my missing ring." It had disappeared after the séance.

"And of course you think I took it."

Anna shrugged. "Kind of."

"Yeah, I just happened to steal a ring that I would never be caught dead wearing."

"Obviously my mom or your dad didn't take it, so that leaves just you."

"Or your friend."

"Eden?"

"I bet she's not as innocent as she would like everyone to think. After all, she is Olivia's twin," Tabitha said with a smirk.

Anna shook her head. "Whatever. Eden wouldn't do that. What else do you want? I didn't go in your room."

"Maybe your mom cleaned my bathroom, then," Tabitha muttered, more to herself than Anna.

"Why would my mom clean your bathroom?" Anna's mom never cleaned up after Anna. She was big on making Anna take responsibility for her room and her laundry.

Tabitha shrugged. "She did last week. I was practically suffocating with the lemon-scented cleaner she used."

Anna seethed. Her mom always made her clean her own bathroom. What made Tabitha so special that she wouldn't have the same rule for her?

"Just stay out of my room," Tabitha said before slamming the door behind her.

"No problem!" Anna shouted to the closed door.

Anna looked down at the thread of texts that had popped up during Tabitha's visit. But then it hit her.

"Wait a minute!" Anna jumped up. "Lemons?" If the smell of lemons was in the air, she knew without a doubt it had to be Lucy. And Lucy was lingering around Tabitha's room. But why?

Anna ran out of her room and down the stairs, two at a time, to the second floor and froze in front of Tabitha's open bedroom door. Harper was in there, her back to Anna. And she was talking to herself.

Anna crept closer, listening.

"Yes," Harper whispered. "That's exactly what I thought." Harper nodded several times. "But how do I do that?"

Silence.

"Are you sure that will work?" More silence. "What?" She spun around and faced Anna. "How long have you been standing there?"

"How long have you been talking to yourself?"

"I'm not talking to myself."

"Right. How long have you been talking to Lucy?"

Harper's face froze.

"C'mon, Lucy," Anna yelled out to the air. "I know why you're not showing yourself to me. Stop being a coward."

"I don't know what you're talking about," Harper said without much conviction. "You should leave now." She pointed to the door.

A silver glint drew Anna's gaze to her finger.

"My ring!" Anna closed the distance between them in three steps and grabbed Harper's finger.

"What? You're crazy! This is mine!"

"No. You took it," Anna said as she struggled to pull the ring off her finger, "and it has my initials engraved inside, so—"

She grunted as she continued to play tug-of-war

with Harper's finger. She pulled harder and still the ring wouldn't budge. "Why ... won't ... this ... come ... *off*!" And with that last word the ring came off. And so did Harper's finger.

Anna squealed and dropped the finger as if it were on fire.

"Great!" Harper shouted as she quickly snatched her finger off the floor. "You just had to pull that finger off. I hope it will reattach again!"

"Again? This happened before?"

Harper shook her head, annoyed. She managed to put her finger back on just as Tabitha walked in with two glasses of juice.

"Anna, what are you doing?" Tabitha asked between clenched teeth. She set the glasses of juice down on the side table next to her and glared at Anna.

"I came to talk to Harper."

"Yep," Harper said, shoving her hand in her pocket. "She came down here and accused me of stealing her ring."

"Oh my God, Anna!" Tabitha shrieked. "Nobody has your stupid ring, so drop it already!"

"She has it!" Anna cried. "She's the one who took it!"

Harper shook her head.

"Look at her hand! She's wearing it!" Anna pointed

to Harper. If Harper was throwing her under the bus, then she would do the same.

"You're crazy." Harper glared at Anna but made no move to take her hand out of her pocket.

"Just show her your hand to prove her wrong so she will finally leave," Tabitha said to Harper.

Harper looked nervous, but she took her hand out. Five fingers. No ring.

"Look in her pocket!" Anna reached over but Tabitha slapped her hand away.

"First you accuse me of stealing, then you accuse my friend. Get out of my room!"

Anna stormed out. The scent of lemons followed her all the way back to her room, but Lucy never appeared.

CHAPTER 21

ANNA

The next morning, Anna got a text from Eden to meet her outside near the teacher's parking lot. "Look what I made!" Eden said when Anna got there, grinning and holding out a cupcake.

"Nice," Anna said. "You've started to bake now?"

"Well, not exactly."

Anna raised a brow.

"I might have conjured this up," Eden whispered.

"So it's a magic cupcake. Will I shrink to the size of an ant if I eat it?" Anna laughed.

"No! But it might help a certain someone remember certain things if he eats it," Eden said.

"What?" Anna exclaimed. "No. That's not the memory cake, right?" Anna frowned at Eden. "I never agreed to it."

"Anna, I know."

"Know what?" Anna asked.

"The real reason why you don't want Johnny to remember."

Anna shook her head. "Of course I want him to remember. I just—"

"Don't want him to remember everything?" Eden finished.

Anna looked into Eden's eyes and slowly nodded.

"I tried the memory spell on myself first," Eden told her. "I thought maybe I would just remember some old childhood memories or something. But I remembered . . . other stuff too." Eden scuffed the toe of her boot into the sidewalk, scraping it back and forth.

"What did you remember?" Anna's voice was barely above a whisper. A huge knot formed in the pit of her stomach. She knew the answer before Eden even said it.

"I know it was me that night, not Olivia."

Anna swallowed. "Yeah."

"What do I do with that information?" Eden asked.

Anna shrugged. "What do you want to do with it?"

"You know the right thing would be to tell Olivia the truth."

Anna looked down at her shoes, shoving her hands in her pockets. She had a lump in her throat the size of a bowling ball.

"I know you were just trying to protect me. I'm not mad."

Anna lifted her head to meet Eden's gaze. "Really?"

"Really. But we'll figure out what to do about all that later. Right now we have this delicious-looking cupcake waiting to be delivered."

Anna couldn't help but smile as she eyeballed the cupcake. Who could resist a chocolate cupcake with fudge frosting loaded with colorful sprinkles? "So that's . . . *it*?"

"Yep." Eden smiled at her creation. "And don't touch!" She playfully slapped Anna's hand away.

"Oh, come on. What harm would a finger of frosting do?"

"A lot." Eden's voice took on that serious tone she had whenever she talked about her craft. "See those sprinkles?"

Anna nodded.

"Those are actually memories of each of us."

Anna's eyebrows shot up. "Huh?"

"Okay, so the pink sprinkles represent the memories

of you. The yellow ones are the memories of me. And the red sprinkles are Lucy, and the green are Olivia, and so on. So as long as he eats all of it, he will have all those memories of us again. Otherwise, there will be huge holes and none of the memories will make any sense."

"So he'll remember everything up till the night of the accident?" Anna asked, staring at the sprinkles.

"Yeah. Are you sure you want him to know about your secrets?"

"Can he remember me *without* my secrets?"

Eden shook her head. "Nope. Doesn't work like that. I can't just pick and choose. He either remembers or he doesn't."

"Okay then." She chewed on her bottom lip. "Are you sure this will work?"

"Absolutely. Piece of cake. Literally."

Anna groaned. "So when are you giving it to Johnny?"

Eden held the cupcake in front of Anna. "I'm not giving it to him. You are."

Anna's eyes grew big. "Wait . . . why me?"

"I'm sure he'd rather get a cupcake from you than me. Plus, he might think you know how to bake."

"Ha-ha, very funny." Anna grabbed the cupcake. The first bell was going to ring any minute. "Fine. I'll give it to him at lunch."

Eden winked. "Great. Can't wait!"

Anna's stomach churned, but why, she wasn't sure. She should be excited that Johnny would remember her, really remember her and their friendship. Shouldn't she?

CHAPTER 22

Harper

"That cupcake looks amazing, Johnny." Tabitha batted her eyes as she leaned against the locker next to his. He was grabbing books out of his locker. Next to him was a beat-up backpack, and next to that was a white paper plate with a chocolate cupcake.

"We can get our own cupcakes, Tabitha. C'mon." Harper grabbed Tabitha's elbow. School was out and she wanted to leave, not hang around while Tabitha made googly eyes at Johnny. She had no idea what the fascination with Johnny was and why every girl seemed to melt just being around him. But whatever it was, she was immune to it.

"You want it?" Johnny offered. "I have to cut back on sugar. Getting ready for our big game coming up."

"Really?" Tabitha said. "You're giving me your cupcake?"

"It's just a cupcake," Harper muttered.

Tabitha either didn't hear her or ignored her comment. She kept talking to Johnny.

"Really, I couldn't take it," Tabitha said, giggling. "Unless you insist."

Johnny nodded to the cupcake. "Go ahead. I'm sure Anna wouldn't mind."

"What does Anna have to do with it?" Tabitha retracted her hand as if the cupcake were poison.

"She's the one who made it for me. She's great, isn't she?"

"Yeah, freakin' fantastic," Tabitha grumbled.

"What?"

Tabitha plastered a plastic smile on her face. "I said yeah, she's fantastic."

Johnny tossed a novel into his backpack and slung it over his shoulder. "So, you want it? I gotta get to practice."

"I'll be outside," Harper said. She couldn't hide her irritation as she walked away, feeling sick from the PDG—public display of grossness. She stopped midstep. Or maybe she was feeling sick for other reasons. She looked down at her hands, loaded with rings. Each of her fingers had fallen off and had had to be reattached. Luckily, she'd scrounged together eight rings, and was using them to conceal the reconnection lines.

Her legs felt as if they were falling asleep. She wiggled her right, then her left. Nothing. They were beginning to feel like deadweight.

Harper continued walking until she got to the parking lot and stood in front of the Academy library with her arms crossed. She wasn't going to wait around all day for Tabitha. A few more minutes and she'd be outta there.

Her back felt tight, as if she could feel her muscles knotting. Had she really been that tense lately? She swiveled her head from front to back, and was rolling out her shoulders when she heard an awful crack.

"What the—"

She brought her hand up to her neck, feeling along the skin until she touched a rough area. It felt jagged. Then her hand dipped into a hollow spot that felt like a hole. It didn't hurt, so she stuck her finger in to further explore. Her finger touched something squishy. Something . . . stringy?

She pulled her hand away quickly and dug in her purse for her compact mirror. She gasped as she saw that her neck was split open. Had it torn from her simple gesture when she was stretching?

She pushed her head slightly to the other side,

trying to balance everything out and make it look straight. The jagged pieces attached, but a very visible line was showing. Much more noticeable than any of the lines on the eight fingers she had had to reattach.

"Good God! I'm turning into Frankenstein." Harper attempted to dab powder from her compact over the line, but it did nothing to conceal the rupture. If anything, it stuck to it and made it look even more unnatural. And even more visible.

"Why didn't I wear a turtleneck today?" she mumbled, tugging up the collar of the green flannel shirt she'd worn instead.

Harper let out a sigh and looked to make sure no one was paying any attention to her. She had to leave before Tabitha saw her. Or anyone else, for that matter. She took off at a sprint. Or rather, that's what she was going for. Instead it looked more like a hop as she tripped over her own feet. Luckily, she stopped herself from falling. Still, her legs felt heavy, and it took every ounce of energy she had to drag herself down the sidewalk. There was no way she could make it back to Anna's house.

She really didn't want to, but she texted Anna.

Need a ride home.

Good luck.

> I'm serious. I can barely walk.
>
> Maybe you should ask your BFF for help.
>
> You want her to know my secret?

Harper could practically hear the sigh from Anna as there was a longer-than-normal pause between texts.

> Where are you?
>
> Down street from library.
>
> Eden and her dad will pick you up.

Harper heard a click-clack of heels echo across the parking lot. Her first instinct was to look over her shoulder, but she was afraid of losing her head. Literally.

She limped over to a nearby house, hiding along the bushes on the side. Tabitha was walking toward the parking lot, her head down, her eyes focused on her phone. Harper's phone, which was still on vibrate from school, went off in her hand. It was a text from Tabitha.

> Where are you?
>
> I left. You were taking too long.
>
> Whatever.

She could practically hear Tabitha seething on the other end. That girl wasn't used to someone telling her no or ditching her. But she'd get over it.

She texted Anna. Her hands were shaking.

You need to help me, Anna. Please.

A few minutes later came Anna's response.

Come up to my room when you get back to the house. Maybe I have a necklace that will help.

Harper felt a wave of relief wash over her.

OK. Thanks. But you're not gonna, like, accuse me of stealing it or something?

Don't be ungrateful, just shut up and wear it.

CHAPTER 23

ANNA

When Harper had arrived home after school, Anna
had given her a black velvet choker necklace. Harper
had scurried off to try it on, and now Anna was downstairs in the living room brainstorming with Eden.
Anna's mom was outside looking at the gutters with
Winston. Apparently there were leaves in the gutters
and it was going to cost a fortune to get them cleaned
because the house was so huge. In any case, her mom
was preoccupied, which meant now was the perfect
time to plan her next step with Eden.

"Why do you look so nervous?" Anna watched as
Eden paced across her living room floor, wearing a
path in the rug.

Eden bit her bottom lip. "I'm not nervous. I'm just . . . thinking."

"That's just as bad."

Eden stopped pacing as Harper rushed into the room.

"You guys need to figure out what's going on with me before I'm forced to wear any more of this so-called jewelry." She looked straight at Anna. "It doesn't even sparkle!"

"Get out of here." Anna threw a pillow at Harper but she caught it in midair.

"Really? You could have seriously decapitated me or something." Harper threw the pillow to the side. "So are you going to help me or not?"

"Not," Eden giggled.

"This isn't funny!" Harper tried to cross her arms, but her wrist bent at an abnormal angle.

"It kinda is," Anna joked. "Now will you please just leave?"

"Not until you agree to help me."

"Fine! Now go."

"Okay, all right, I'm leaving."

As Harper stormed off, Millie popped into the room, appearing beside Anna.

"Okay." Millie clapped her hands together. "So what's this plan to get rid of Tabitha and how can I help?"

"What if there was a way to fix both of my problems at once?" Anna asked.

"Go on," Eden said.

"Yeah. What if we could get Tabitha to move out and back home with her mom, and get Harper to finally vacate her body and move on?"

"I'm up for it," Millie said. "What did you have in mind?"

"Well . . . ," Anna asked slowly. "What if we make sure Tabitha is around to see Harper break a leg off, or reattach an ear or something?"

"But if she says something—" Eden started.

"No one will believe her," Anna said.

"Plus," Eden said, "I could always do a spell to make her forget what she saw."

"No, that would defeat the whole purpose of this," Anna pointed out. "She has to remember so she'll go running for the hills. Or the city. You know."

"How will that get rid of Harper?" Millie asked.

"I've noticed that she has more of these incidents when she's outside," Anna told them. "The sun must speed up the process or something. So if we can keep her outside, maybe she'll just keep falling apart until she has no other choice but to leave?"

It was as good a plan as any. Anna only hoped it would work.

CHAPTER 24
ANNA

What is this? Anna blew a dozen layers of dust off the top of the long, skinny box. She was amazed how many secrets the Manor library held. Each time she visited, she discovered things she had somehow missed before. It was almost as if things kept . . . appearing.

Anna sat on the floor with the box, lifting the lid.

A Ouija board.

She grabbed the heavy board and set it with a thump on the floor in front of her. She'd seen Ouija boards before, but she'd never seen one like this. It was made of solid wood, not cardboard. It was in good condition—it looked new, in fact—but at the same time, it felt like something that had been around a long time. It was decorated with the letters of the alphabet, the numbers 0 to 9, and the words YES and NO. She had never played with one before. Who really believed in all that spirit stuff?

"I guess I do now," Anna said to herself.

The heart-shaped wooden planchette, which was designed to move over the board and indicate messages from spirits, was large and heavy. Anna ran her hand along the surface.

Anna moved the empty box to the side and a piece of paper fluttered out, settling by her feet.

A warning.

> *This is not a game. This could have serious*
> *consequences.*
> *Always use in numbers.*
> *Never invite unwanted spirits in.*

It was handwritten in ink. The curly letters and dips gave it an ominous feel.

The library door was suddenly thrown open. "Hey, sis."

Anna nearly jumped out of her skin. She quickly pushed the board under the chair behind her.

"What's going on?" Tabitha walked into the room and looked Anna up and down.

"Nothing." Anna stood with her arms crossed. She knew Tabitha wouldn't be in here, let alone speak to her, if she didn't have a motive.

"Nothing, huh?" Tabitha tilted her head, looking suspiciously at Anna.

Anna watched her eyes survey the room. *Please don't notice the box. Please don't notice the box.*

Maybe it was the silent plea that somehow alerted Tabitha, but her glance fell to the floor and settled on the box. A smile broke out across her face as her eyes darted between Anna and the box.

"What's that?" Tabitha pointed.

Anna shrugged as Tabitha crossed the room. She picked up the empty box with a look of disappointment. Then her gaze flicked to the chair. And to the board underneath.

"Oh, look!" Tabitha feigned surprise. "A Ouija board." She picked it up. "I haven't played with one of these since fourth grade."

"I wasn't playing with it," Anna mumbled.

"Sure. Of course you weren't. You were just getting it ready. For your next little slumber party. Right?"

Anna wished she could slap the sarcastic tone right out of her.

"You know, silence is the same as admitting guilt."

"What do you want, Tabitha?"

"Your mom wants to talk to you. She's on the back patio. She asked me to come and find you."

Great. Anna walked out of the room, leaving Tabitha alone with the Ouija board.

. . .

Anna found her mom on the patio, but she wasn't alone. Winston occupied the chair next to her. When Anna stepped outside, he stood up. "You can have my seat, Annabel. I've got some pruning to take care of." He headed off toward the garage.

She could feel her mouth twist into a scowl. She hoped her mom didn't notice.

"Sit, sit. Let's chat." Her mom beamed. There was a plate with crackers and grapes on it, and some little napkins that said *Celebrate!*

Anna sat and glared.

"What's wrong, honey?"

"Nothing."

"Annabel." Her mom made her name sound like a warning.

"Fine. I don't like them living here."

"Honey, this is their new home now." She frowned

and glanced toward the cemetery. "Isn't it beautiful out here?"

"It's a cemetery, Mom."

"But it's landscaped so beautifully. And it's so peaceful."

"Because it's a cemetery."

"You know why I like doing the hair and makeup over there for Winston?"

Anna shook her head. She looked down at her hands as she tore a napkin into tiny pieces. The napkin was just like her life.

"Because," her mom started, waiting for Anna to look up. "Sometimes the dead are more pleasant than the living."

Anna snorted. "That's so morbid, Mom."

"But it's true. They are quiet. They don't complain and they sit very still." Her mom chuckled.

"And they don't tip," Anna pointed out.

"It's not always about the money. You have to enjoy what you do."

Her mom patted her arm once and leaned back. "It will get better. You'll see. Everyone just needs time to adjust."

"Yeah, right," Anna muttered.

The corners of her mom's mouth curved down. "I know it was always me and you. It will still always be me and you. But now we have Winston and Tabitha. You should get to know her better."

"You barely know her either." Anna's stomach churned.

"I know, but I'm trying to make time and change that." Her mom sighed. "Maybe your new friend Eden isn't such a good friend for you. Tabitha has told me stories. You should try to hang out more with her friends. Like Harper."

Anna stared at her. "Are you serious? You're going to believe whatever she tells you?"

"She has no reason to lie, honey."

Anna couldn't take it anymore. She pushed her chair back and ran up to her room.

CHAPTER 25
ANNA

Anna lay on her bed listening to music and feeling sorry for herself until it was dark. No one had called her for dinner. They probably hadn't even noticed she wasn't there. She opened her door and headed downstairs. The whole place was silent. Eerie. Her footsteps echoed in the hallways.

When she went into the kitchen, Winston was pouring himself a cup of tea. "Hey there, Annabel."

"Hey," she said, opening the refrigerator. She took out a cheese stick and an apple. Maybe she'd make herself a cup of instant soup.

"Now, Annabel, just because we have a housekeeper now doesn't mean you shouldn't pick up after yourself."

"Housekeeper?" Anna clutched the apple. She was always the last to know. Her mom had never hired someone to clean up after them.

"Just because someone is getting paid to clean the Manor doesn't mean you should get careless. I don't want Tabitha learning these behaviors from you, either."

Anna's mouth fell open. She snapped it closed before any comments came tumbling out that she would regret later.

Instead of saying anything, she spun on her heel and headed to the Manor's library and called Eden to vent. Even over the phone, Eden was able to calm her down.

After mentioning the Ouija board to Eden, she suggested they use it as attempt number two to contact Uncle Maxwell.

"We should do it in the cemetery. By his grave," Eden said.

"At midnight during a full moon, right?" Anna was done with the stereotypical approaches. The séance was proof of how well that stuff didn't work.

"Funny. Let's do it tomorrow night."

"Okay." Anna sighed. Hopefully, they'd have better luck this time.

Anna looked for the Ouija board on the library

shelves and under the chair where she had left it when Tabitha came in, but it was gone. Of course Tabitha hadn't put it back where it was supposed to go.

In fact, it didn't seem she'd put it back anywhere in that room. Had Tabitha hidden it?

Anna texted Eden.

> Ouija board gone. Don't know where Tabitha put it.
>
> And you don't want to ask, right?
>
> Right.
>
> OK, I'll come over in the morning and do a locator spell.
>
> Thanks ☺

Anna showered, then sat down on her bed and looked at her phone. It beeped continuously. A handful of texts from new deadies and two from Mary. The girl looking for her body.

> I think it might be buried already.
>
> It can't be buried!!!

Anna texted back.

I'll help you figure this out, it will be OK.

OMG thank you! You're the best!

"Why can't they all be like that?" Anna muttered.

The last text was from Spencer. He was at the clubhouse.

Yo, Tabitha and Harper are here too.

A sudden idea hit Anna. She sent a text back to Spencer.

Keep an eye on Tabitha for me and let me know when she leaves. Important!

Anna tossed the phone on her bed and ran downstairs to Tabitha's room. She was in such a rush she didn't hear Spencer text her back only seconds later.

Tabitha left a while ago.

CHAPTER 26
ANNA

There was nothing wrong with searching someone's room if you were only there to look for something they took from you, right? Anna assured herself she had every right to search through Tabitha's stuff. She just wished the room were smaller. She wasn't sure where to even begin.

If I were Tabitha, where would I hide a Ouija board? Anna wondered.

Anna checked under Tabitha's bed. No luck.

She checked under her mattress. Nope. And in the massive oak dresser, in the bathroom (which had a sitting area), and around the bookshelf, but no Ouija board.

Finally she decided to check the walk-in closet. *How can one girl wear SO many clothes?* Anna made her way through the cashmere sweater jungle and past the shelves stocked with shoes from floor to ceiling. When she stopped in front of the revolving accessory compartments, she heard voices. Anna froze as she strained to hear.

It was Tabitha and Harper.

Anna's heart pounded frantically as she reached in her back pocket for her phone. It wasn't there. She patted down her other pockets, afraid she'd dropped it somewhere in Tabitha's room. Wait. She remembered—she'd left it in her own room.

She mentally smacked herself for pulling such a stupid move. Of course she needed her phone if Spencer was going to keep tabs on Tabitha for her.

The voices became louder until they were right outside the bedroom. There was no time to escape. They would see her for sure. Panic seized Anna. How did she get herself into situations like this? She surveyed the clothing prison, searching for somewhere to hide.

Just past the revolving accessory compartments were a full-size vanity and a dressing area. Anna shook her head. No, still too exposed. To her right was a luggage set, ranging in size from super tiny to large enough to fit an entire apartment's worth of stuff.

Anna opted for a midsize piece and unzipped it. The inside wasn't empty like she had been hoping. Several rolled-up blankets were stashed in there, taking up all the space. Anna pushed that suitcase to the side as she heard Tabitha talking right outside the closet door now. Grabbing the largest suitcase, which was thankfully empty, she climbed inside and rolled her body into the space. She didn't bother zipping herself in but held the top down instead. As she did, she noticed something on the floor across from her. Under the vanity.

The Ouija board.

I knew it! It wasn't in the box, though, and the planchette was lying on it and two candles were sitting beside it. It looked as if it had been . . . used?

Anna didn't have time to think any more about it as the closet door opened and footsteps walked toward her before finally coming to an abrupt halt in front of the luggage where Anna hid.

CHAPTER 27
ANNA

"Where is it?" Harper yelled.

"By the shoes!" Tabitha's voice rang out from a distance.

"It's not by the shoes!" Harper yelled back.

Anna peeked through a small gap. Harper was searching the closet for something. But what?

"Try by the luggage!"

Anna sucked in a gasp and closed her eyes. Because maybe if she didn't see Harper, then Harper wouldn't notice her. It was reasonable enough. If only she had her phone, she could have Eden cause a distraction that would free her from this mess.

If only she had her phone, she wouldn't be in this situation in the first place.

Her thoughts distracted her from Harper, who must've left at some point, because the only sound Anna heard now was her heart pounding. She could feel sweat beading on her forehead, her leg was cramping, and she was beginning to feel slightly claustrophobic.

Making small, quiet movements, Anna slowly pushed the top up.

"See! I told you it was here!" Tabitha shouted.

Anna froze. Tabitha was in front of her.

"You said by the shoes. That is not by the shoes."

"I said vanity! Get your ears checked."

The vanity? Were they talking about the Ouija board?

"It's not like I'm the one who freaked out and almost lit the carpet on fire!" Harper said.

"Well, it's not like I'm the one who invited evil dead things into my room."

"You can't seriously believe that."

"Are you kidding? You've seen the stuff that's been happening. The noises late at night. The footsteps and creaky doors."

Harper sighed loudly. "Well, it was your idea to play with the stupid thing."

"I just wanted to see what the big deal was. Anna is so immature. Just put this in her room and maybe the ghosts or whatever will leave me alone and haunt her instead."

"Why do I have to do it?"

"Because I don't want to."

"I don't want to either."

"Look, I don't need her hanging something over my head. She likes you a lot better than me. So just do it and quit complaining."

Anna heard the closet door close and the padding of footsteps walking away. She stayed crouched where she was until she saw the sliver of light under the door turn dark.

CHAPTER 28

Harper

Harper wasn't sure why, but lately her cravings were changing. She found it impossible to get full and her stomach was always rumbling. She wrote down her frustrations in her journal.

> *I better not gain a ton of weight from all this eating. Is that even possible?*

Not only that, but she was beyond tired. She fell asleep in class and was clumsy. Even more so than Anna.

> *If I trip over my own feet one more time, I swear I'll scream.*

With that last sentence, Harper's pen slipped from her grip and fell to the floor. She grunted as she picked it up, then slammed her notebook shut. Her brain was also foggy, and it seemed to be getting worse with each passing day.

When Eden came over the following morning to do the locator spell, Harper cornered her and Anna. "So why is this happening?" Harper looked back and forth between them, searching their faces for answers.

"Not sure what you mean." Eden pushed past Harper as she followed Anna outside. They entered the cemetery. "But we have things to do and—"

"Oh, I forgot to tell you," Anna interrupted. "I found it. So we don't really have things to do anymore."

Harper followed close behind. "I'm serious. I want answers!"

"What are we talking about?" Eden sounded annoyed.

"Don't act like you don't know," Harper said. "You were supposed to find out why all this is happening to me."

"I'm not exactly a ghost doctor," Eden said, "but it sounds like you're falling apart."

"Falling to pieces, actually," Anna added.

"That still doesn't tell me anything. What's. Going. On?" Harper drew out the sentence very slowly.

"You know how you died before?" Anna said. "Well, when you reentered your body, you had control over it, but physically your body was still . . . dead."

"So what?" Harper said, feeling panicky. "I was fine at first. This falling-apart stuff only started happening recently."

"My guess is the solutions that were put in your body before you were buried helped to preserve your body for a little while," Anna said. "But with constant exposure to the outside world and regaining use, it started the decaying process."

"Yeah, the preservatives only helped to delay the inevitable. It was only a matter of time before your body started falling apart," Eden said.

"But Lucy said I would be alive!" Harper protested.

"Well, you are," Anna said. She scraped at some moss that had formed on a large tombstone. "You just weren't meant to stay that way." She shot Harper a look. "I warned you about Lucy too. You dug your own grave. Now you need to lie in it."

"Very funny." Harper stumbled. Her right foot had spun around and was now pointing in the wrong direction: backwards.

"Oh!" Harper reached down to grab her foot. "What do I need to do to stop this?" She twisted her ankle around so that her foot was facing in the right direction.

"You need to leave your body," Anna said, shrugging.

"So I have to look for another body again?"

"What do you mean, *again*?" Eden asked.

Harper waved the question away. "You know, I got into this body once, I don't want to have to do that again."

"You can't do it again, Harper," Anna said softly. "You have to leave your body and then—"

"And then what?" Harper demanded. "I just sit here all bored and invisible until some ghostly Prince Charming whisks me away into the cemetery, like Lucy?"

"You'll go wherever you're supposed to go," Anna said. "Follow the natural order of things."

"Gee, thanks for so much useful information. Now I know exactly what to do."

"I never said I have all the answers," Anna said quietly. "I'm just a girl with a cell phone and an iPad. And it's not for me to know where spirits go when they leave this world. For all I know, you could be headed to a very hot location."

Eden let out a giggle, which only infuriated Harper more.

"Why can't you cast some spell, witchy girl? Solve all our problems."

"I don't use dark magic," Eden said firmly. "Doing any kind of spell to interfere with a spirit and a body is prohibited."

"I promise not to tell your witchy coven or whatever. Just do it."

Eden shook her head. "Once I let the darkness in, it could take over. I can't take that chance. It could cost other people their lives too."

"So you're saying I'm not important enough to risk that?" Harper asked, her voice rising to a high-pitched squeak.

"Exactly. Wait, no. Not just you, but anybody."

"So if Anna had this problem, you wouldn't help her either?"

"No," Eden whispered. She gave Anna an apologetic look.

Anna shrugged. "Not like I would ever make the kind of choices you did and end up in a position like this anyway."

"Have you figured out who pushed me off that balcony yet?" Harper asked.

Anna shook her head. "Not yet."

"You suck at this investigating stuff." Harper grabbed Eden's Spell Phone out of her hand. "Let me check and make sure there isn't anything else that you can do to help me."

"Give that back." Eden reached for it but Harper held it away from her.

"Oh, look at this. . . ." Harper stepped back with a smug look. "It says here that a body can remain intact as long as the deteriorating brain is supplemented."

Eden and Anna froze.

"Wait, so my brain is deteriorating? That's why I can't think or . . . or . . . you know, find missing words?"

"Yes, but that's not all of it—"

"So all I have to do is use another brain and I can stay alive."

"No!" Anna and Eden shouted at the same time.

Harper's lips curved into a smile. "You just don't want me to stay alive. That's the real reason. Isn't it?"

"Even with another brain, your body will still fall apart."

"But that would buy me more time. To find a way out of this. I can just visit your stepfather at the funeral home tonight. I'm sure I won't have any problem finding a brain there."

"But any brain you find there will be dead," Anna told her. "It won't work."

"Anna!" Eden elbowed Anna in her side. "Why'd you have to tell her that?"

"Ohhhh, so it has to be from someone still alive?" Harper looked up toward the sky as she thought about this.

"So if I actually get a brain, what do I do with it? Won't it mess up my hair if I try to put a brain inside my head?" She eyed Anna very carefully.

Anna bit her bottom lip, swaying back and forth. She was holding back.

Harper searched Eden's face. She was trying very carefully to keep her expression blank.

"I have to eat it, is that it? Eat brains like in those zombie movies?"

Harper watched both Anna's and Eden's eyes practically pop out of their heads.

Harper smiled. "That's it. I figured it out and didn't even have to use my entire brain to do that." Her insides churned at the very thought of ingesting brain food. "You guys suck at keeping secrets too."

CHAPTER 29

Harper

"Something really strange is going on," Tabitha said later that day as she picked at the grass. It was a warm afternoon, and she and Harper were soaking up the sun's rays at the village park. But Tabitha couldn't suppress a shiver.

"Strange?" Harper wondered if her friend knew the secret of her undead life. Or that Anna communicated with ghosts. Or that Eden was a witch. Or—

"It's like I know things that I shouldn't."

Or something like that.

"What do you mean?" Harper asked.

"I thought I was just having weird dreams, but they are so real. And I can remember every detail of every dream. Actually, I can't forget them. So it's like a memory but there's no way I would know this stuff."

"Hmmm." Harper wondered if Eden wasn't the only witch in town.

"Is that a good 'hmmm' or a bad 'hmmm'?"

"Neither." Harper wondered if a certain someone had cast a spell over her friend. "What kind of things are you remembering?"

Tabitha picked a dandelion. "Stuff about Anna. And Johnny."

Harper sat up. "What kind of stuff?"

"Well, like the accident with Johnny is different than what everyone says happened."

Eden definitely hadn't cast a spell on her then.

"How do you think it happened?"

"I'm not exactly sure, since it doesn't all make sense, but one of the twins was there. And they swung at Anna but missed and clocked Johnny instead. Johnny crashed through the glass table. Then lots of screaming and then one of the Ashbury twins went hysterical and Anna kept yelling 'Lucy!'"

"That's really weird."

"Do you know a Lucy?" Tabitha asked.

Harper thought for a second before speaking.

"Yeah. There was a girl named Lucy who used to go to the Academy."

"What happened to her? She moved?"

Harper didn't want to give away too much info, since she was supposedly just as new to the area as Tabitha.

"I'm not exactly sure, but gossip around the school is that she had an accident."

"An accident?"

Harper shrugged. "I guess."

"So it happened at the same time as Johnny?"

"No, this was before. She hit her head. In the cemetery."

Tabitha gasped. "Is she okay?"

Harper shook her head.

Tabitha opened her hand and looked down at the dandelion she'd crushed in her palm. The fluffy bits wafted away on the slight breeze. "Wanna head up to the Corner Café and get a burger and fries?"

"Sure. Sounds great." Harper forced a tiny smile. What was wrong with her? A burger and fries sounded absolutely disgusting. She wanted something juicy, like a steak. But rare. Like, really, really rare. Or even uncooked. Kind of like . . . a brain?

Harper couldn't help salivating at the very thought. She shook her head furiously, trying to get the images out of her head.

"Harper? You ready?"

"What? Oh yeah. Sure."

Harper walked close to Tabitha, noticing a new, unfamiliar scent. "New shampoo?"

"Nope. Same as always."

Hmmm. Harper wondered what this new scent coming from the tip-top of Tabitha's head could be, even though deep down inside, she already knew the answer.

CHAPTER 30
ANNA

"So she knows?" Anna asked Harper later that day. Tabitha was at a dentist appointment with Anna's mom, and Anna, Eden, and Harper were at the kitchen table. "How does Tabitha know anything about that night? You must have told her something."

"No, I swear," Harper said. "And how would I even know anything about that night?"

"We know you talked to Lucy," Eden said.

"But I haven't. Not really," Harper said.

"Or maybe you have but you can't remember. Because your brain is disappearing. Hello! Ever think of that?" Anna couldn't help raising her voice. She didn't do well with news like this. She always crumbled under bad situations. Or news.

"I think I would remember something like that. But apparently Tabitha remembers."

"She can't. She wasn't even there," Eden said.

"That's the thing," Harper said. "She says she has these dreams and she remembers them. All of them. So they are kind of like memories. She says they're so real and—"

"Wait." Eden held up her hand. "What did you just say?"

"How she remembers all of them," Harper said.

Eden shook her head. "No, about memories."

Anna gasped as she caught on to what Eden was thinking.

"Tabitha said they seemed more like memories than dreams, but had no idea how that could be," Harper said.

"I know how." Eden looked at Anna. "She ate the cupcake."

"She ate the cupcake? Is that a code? What does that mean?" Harper looked back and forth between Anna and Eden, but they ignored her.

"No way. She couldn't have. I mean, if she did— Oh no. You really think so?" Anna said.

"It would make more sense if she did," Eden said.

Anna stood up. "Can you stop being so calm for once and actually freak out? I don't want to be the only one having all these freak-out moments."

"Can someone please tell me what is going on?" Harper yelled.

Anna and Eden abruptly turned to Harper, as if just now remembering she was in the room with them.

"Eden made a memory cake," Anna told her. "It was a cupcake with a spell. I gave it to Johnny so he'd eat it and regain the memories he lost before the accident."

Harper's eyes widened. "So if Johnny didn't eat the cupcake and someone else did . . ." Her voice trailed off.

"Then that person would get those memories," Eden finished.

Harper laughed. "Pretty sure Tabitha did eat the cupcake."

Both Anna and Eden stared at Harper as if her arm had just fallen off. Which wasn't all that remote a possibility.

"And how exactly do you know that?" Anna questioned.

"Because I was with her when Johnny offered it to her."

"Did she eat the whole thing? Or only part of it?" Eden asked.

"And what color were the sprinkles she ate?" Anna blurted out.

Harper frowned. "I have no idea. I took off before she ate it. That was when, you know, I started falling apart that day."

Anna scooted closer to Harper. "So there's a chance she *didn't* eat it?"

"Nope. I'm pretty sure she did. She would've eaten a worm if Johnny offered it to her. Speaking of worms . . . I'm kind of hungry—"

"What does this mean, Eden?" Anna asked worriedly. "Tabitha knows about us now?"

"Probably. But that's not the worst part."

"How is that not the worst part? She'll use this against us. My secret will be out. Your secret will be out!"

"I think the side effects to this spell are pretty bad if taken by someone other than the intended," Eden said, looking something up on her phone. "Her brain won't have room to store all these extra memories, so it will grow."

"Her brain will grow? That doesn't sound too bad." Anna sat back down.

"Except it won't stop growing. When memories are implanted in someone who doesn't have the vacant space already, the brain will continue expanding. Like a balloon. Until it can't stretch any further and then . . ."

"Her head will explode? You're kidding, right?" Anna asked.

"I wish I were." Eden's hands started to tremble.

"How much time do we have?" Anna asked. This was bad. Definitely bad.

"About forty-eight hours," Eden said.

"Mmmm, brains," Harper said with a smile. "Oh, sorry. Did I say that aloud?"

• • •

Maddsen Manor had been deathly quiet when Anna had put a sweatshirt on over her T-shirt and flannel pj bottoms and tiptoed out of the house.

The cemetery was even quieter. Using her flashlight app, she'd carefully made her way through the tombstones and grass to where her friends were waiting for her.

"There." Anna set the wooden Ouija board down on

the grass and sat next to Eden and Millie on Maxwell Maddsen's grave. It was almost midnight.

"Can't you just call him for us?" Anna asked Millie.

"It's not like there's a ghost network. I can't just summon anyone just because they're dead. It doesn't work like that." Millie said. She touched the Ouija board. "How do we use this?'

Anna let out a sigh. "Have you ever seen one of these, Millie?"

Millie shook her head. "When I was a kid, we played marbles. And jacks."

"Sounds like fun." Eden pretended to snore.

"So we each place a finger on the pointer," Anna began.

"Planchette," Eden corrected.

"Same thing." Anna rolled her eyes. "Anyway, we ask a question and wait for the *planchette* to move."

"But we're supposed to move it with our fingers?" Millie asked, wiggling hers.

"No, the whole point is *not* to move it. We only have our fingers on it to give it our energy to help it move."

Millie shook her head. "Okay, whatever you guys say."

They placed their fingers on the planchette. "Make sure you're not pressing down. Just touch it lightly," Anna said. "And focus all your concentration.

I'll ask first." She kept her eyes closed as she whispered. "We call upon Maxwell Maddsen. Can you hear us?"

Anna didn't feel any movement. She took a deep breath. "Maxwell Maddsen, are you here?"

Nothing.

Don't break concentration, Anna thought.

She felt her body relax, her muscles melt, as she pictured all tension leaving her body. Her shoulders dropped; her body slumped slightly forward.

"Is there anyone here with us?"

Somewhere in the distance they heard an owl. Anna felt Eden jump next to her.

"Is there—"

The pointer began sliding under their fingertips. Anna's eyes popped open. The three girls stared down at the board. It moved over letters, not stopping, then changed direction and glided slowly toward the top of the board.

"Are either of you moving it?" Eden squeaked.

Anna shook her head.

"No," Millie said. "I was gonna ask you the same thing."

It came to the top, stopping on the word YES.

"What do we do now?" Eden looked to Anna.

"Is this Maxwell Maddsen?" Anna asked.

This time it moved much more quickly, stopping at the word NO.

"Should we stop now?" Eden asked. "What if it's something evil?"

Anna breathed in through her nose, concentrating on all the scents around her. A light pine fragrance tickled her nose. "No," Anna said. "It's not evil. Probably just someone who's reaching out for help."

"Tell them to just text you later," Millie whispered.

"Can you sense or see any other spirits, Millie?" Anna knew Millie's powers were far beyond Anna's capabilities.

Millie shook her head. "No. They are completely cloaked. So it's someone who's been gone for a while."

Anna's fingers shook, quivering slightly on the board. "Who is here?" she asked.

The planchette moved to the letter *D* and stopped.

"*D*?" asked Eden.

It moved to the next letter. *A*.

Eden sucked in a sharp breath.

It quickly moved to the third and final letter before stopping. *D*.

"Dad," Anna whispered.

"Dad," Millie echoed.

"Dad?" Eden looked at the two girls. "Whose dad? Mine is at home."

"Mine has been gone a long time, but he could've contacted me anytime he wanted," Millie said softly.

Both heads turned to Anna.

"My dad is . . . he died when I was little. Could it really be *my* dad?" She could barely get the words out. Her heart pounded in her chest; her mouth went dry.

The planchette started moving on the board without anyone touching it. It slid to the word YES.

Anna didn't realize she was crying until her tears splattered on the board. She quickly wiped her eyes. "How . . . I wasn't summoning . . . I mean, what—" She couldn't put a coherent string of words together. Her brain couldn't process fast enough to speak what she was thinking.

But Anna didn't have time to process what was happening. Because a moment later, two things happened simultaneously.

They heard a phone ringing beneath them. In the ground. "What the—?" Eden looked around her, trying to pinpoint the ringing.

And they had an unexpected visitor. A shadow fell over them from behind.

"Isn't anyone gonna answer that?" Archer chuckled.

CHAPTER 31
ANNA

Millie immediately vanished.

"What are you doing here?" Eden asked casually, like it was the most normal thing to be in the grave-yard past midnight. With a Ouija board. At least the ringing phone had stopped.

"Oh, you know," Archer said nervously with a shrug. "Couldn't sleep. Took a walk. What are you guys up to?" He ran his fingers through his thick blond hair. He was wearing a navy

quarter-zip fleece and jeans. Anna noticed he was sweating, his face flushed.

"Same," Eden said, eyeing him.

Anna and Eden exchanged looks and Archer's smile vanished. "Are you guys hiding something?"

Anna watched his face as he looked down and noticed the board. "A Ouija board. Cool! Can I join you guys?"

"Um . . ." Eden was at a loss for words. But Archer sat down between them.

"Who are we trying to communicate with?" he asked.

A sense of dread fell over Anna. She couldn't explain why, but something wasn't right. She knew that much.

When no one answered Archer, he continued. "C'mon, guys, it's not like I ran screaming because of ghosts the last time, right?"

Eden's eyes widened. "Last time?"

"You remember that?" Anna's voice quivered.

"Yeah, was I supposed to forget about it for some reason?" Archer looked directly at Eden.

"It's just, you hadn't mentioned it, so we thought maybe you forgot or something," Eden said.

"Yeah." Anna nodded. She glanced at Eden, who was focusing intently on Archer. *She's casting a memory spell*, Anna realized.

"I'm not stupid, you know." Archer crossed his arms.

"No one ever said you were stupid, Archer." Anna felt like she was talking someone off the ledge. The ledge of what, she wasn't sure. And she didn't want to find out. But she'd do whatever it took to keep his attention focused on her until Eden was finished. She glanced back at Eden.

Eden nodded and mouthed the word "Done."

Anna felt a whoosh of relief wash over her. She stood up, dusting off the back of her jeans. "Hey, Archer. Wanna hang out tomorrow after school?"

"Yeah, let's go to the clubhouse." Eden got up, standing next to Anna.

But Archer didn't stand up. Instead, he yelped, grasping the sides of his head.

"Archer?" Anna stepped forward, touching his arm. "Are you okay?"

Archer slowly put his hands down, never looking away. "Do you have any idea what that feels like?"

"What what feels like?" Anna asked nervously.

"It's like bolts of lightning," Archer continued, ignoring Anna. "Shooting through my brain. Do you know what that feels like? To have electrical currents stabbing you in the head, Anna? Because I do. Thanks to Eden, I've had to go through that wonderful experience several times now."

Anna turned to her friend. "What is he talking about, Eden?"

Eden stood frozen. "The spell."

"Eden!" Anna couldn't believe she'd just said the S-word around Archer.

"He knows, Anna."

"What do you mean, he knows?" Anna looked from Archer to Eden and back to Archer. "What's going on?"

"Why don't you tell her, Eden? Since you're her best friend and all."

"Archer's a warlock," Eden mumbled. She gave Archer a look of defeat. "I swear I didn't know. Not at first."

"But when you found out, you tried to keep Anna away from me, right? Because someone like me doesn't deserve to have friends."

"What are you talking about?" Anna asked Archer. "You both sound crazy!"

"Well, Anna, your best friend here put a spell on you so you would stay away from me."

"What?" Anna spun around and faced Eden. "Is that true?"

"It's not the way it sounds, though. It wasn't—"

"Did you cast a spell on me, Eden?" Anna demanded.

Eden looked away.

"I can't believe you!" Anna's voice echoed through the night air. "You promised you would never do that to me. You were supposed to be my friend."

"I am your friend." Eden's voice was barely above a whisper.

"A friend wouldn't have done that." Anna wanted to run home. But instead she turned away, walking calmly, clutching her phone. And why had Millie ditched her? She'd come here tonight with two friends and was leaving with none.

"I'm sorry, Anna!" Eden called out, but Anna never looked back.

The second Anna got back to Maddsen Manor, she poured herself a glass of water and leaned against the counter, trying to catch her breath. She was still unable to accept what had just happened.

"Anna!" Her mom rushed into the kitchen. "You're home!

Anna jumped, spilling water on the floor.

"Mom! You scared me!" She grabbed a dish towel and started soaking up the mess.

"Do you have any idea how worried I've been?"

"Um . . ."

"How could you think it would be okay to leave the house without telling me?" her mom demanded. "And in the middle of the night!"

"Mom, I'm sorry. I was in the cemetery. I was practically in the backyard!"

"You snuck out, Anna! Do you not think that's a big deal?"

"It's not *that* big a deal," Anna said.

"Just, just go to your room," her mom said through clenched teeth. Her face was bright red. "I'll deal with you tomorrow."

"Mom. It's not like I was out doing anything bad."

"I said go to your room. *Now.*" Her mom was fuming.

"But, Mom . . ."

"Anna!" She pointed her finger at the stairs.

"Fine. All right, I'm going. Geez!" Anna stomped all the way up the stairs, not caring if she woke anyone else up.

CHAPTER 32

ANNA

The next morning, Anna had to drag herself out of bed. She woke up with the worst headache. It wasn't like lightning shooting through her brain, but still. Her head throbbed with the slightest bit of movement, and her energy was at an all-time low. She rummaged through a pile of discarded clothes on her floor and put on her jeans and a striped T-shirt. She felt like she was walking uphill through quicksand.

She saw several text messages from Eden and chose to ignore them, shoving her phone in her back pocket. Then she did a double take as she noticed something sitting on her desk. It was a phone.

Her old phone. The one she had dug a small hole for and had buried when she'd first said goodbye to Millie all those weeks ago.

There was a scratch in the upper corner of the screen. And it was covered in dirt.

This was the phone that they had heard ringing last night in the cemetery.

Millie. She had vanished last night and never returned. Anna gripped the phone tighter. She still needed her. And what about her dad? She couldn't ask Eden to help her contact him again. She needed Millie.

Anna stashed the old phone in the top drawer of her nightstand, then threw her messenger bag over her shoulder and headed downstairs. She was so focused on the steps she almost ran straight into Winston at the bottom of the stairs.

"Whoa!" Anna jumped back. "Sorry, didn't see you." He was blocking the front door and didn't seem to understand she was in a hurry. "I have to leave," she said, and reached around him, hoping he'd move so she could turn the knob, but he didn't. He stared at her with his arms crossed.

"What?" Anna said.

"Heard you snuck out last night."

Anna screamed in her head. She had to get to school. "Mom is talking to me later about it."

"No, I think we need to talk about it now. Go sit down in the living room."

"I have to leave now or I'll be late."

"I'll give you a ride to school."

Anna's heart was pounding. What was she supposed to do? Her mom would not let her be late to school if she were here. He was probably doing this behind her back. She wasn't going to be a part of that.

"No," Anna whispered, looking away.

Winston's eyes widened. "No?"

"I'll talk to Mom later." Anna turned and headed toward the back door. She'd rather walk through the cemetery to get to school than stay at home.

"Where do you think you're going?" Winston called out.

"I'm going to school. Like I'm supposed to," Anna shouted, before slamming the door behind her.

Anna didn't even remember walking to school. She was so deep in her thoughts that the next thing she knew, she looked up and was in the parking lot of the Academy.

"Anna!" Eden ran up to her, falling into step beside her. "Did you get my texts?" She sounded like she had run a marathon as she tried to catch her breath.

"Yep." Anna looked straight ahead as they walked into the building.

"Can you just talk to me for a minute?"

Anna punched in her locker combo and opened the door.

"Stop!" Eden grabbed Anna's arm.

Anna spun around. "What, Eden? What do you want?"

"I just want to talk to you for a minute."

"And if I don't talk to you, are you gonna cast a spell on me?"

"Stop being dumb. You know I wouldn't do something like that if I didn't have a good reason for it."

"Hey, guys, are you two still fighting?" Archer stopped in front of them, smirking.

"Go away, Archer."

"Maybe I don't want him to go away, Eden. Ever think of that?"

"You need to trust me on this. Stay away from him, Anna."

Archer laughed. "Yeah, Anna. Stay away from me. I'm dangerous."

The bell rang for first period. Archer was already gone but Eden wouldn't give up.

"I'm serious, Anna. There are things you don't know."

"Why don't you let me make decisions for myself, okay?" Anna slammed her locker. "Tabitha only has twenty-four hours left, so we still have to work together to help her. Meet me after school. But that's it. After that, I'm done."

CHAPTER 33

Harper

"How is it that now that we need Tabitha, she's suddenly MIA?" Anna asked. She and Eden had cornered Harper in the hallway between classes and they'd scurried over to a dead-end hallway that was used only by the janitorial staff. No one could see them.

Harper shrugged. "How should I know?" But she knew exactly where Tabitha was. She just wasn't about to let Anna get to her before she could. Her appetite was growing at an increasingly alarming rate.

"We have less than twenty-four hours before her head explodes! Don't you get that?" Eden stood only inches from Harper. Finally, the witch had lost her cool.

"She doesn't care," Anna said to Eden. "She wants

this to happen." She turned back to Harper. "She's your friend. Or was. Doesn't that mean anything to you?"

Harper shrugged. "Sure. But sometimes we have to make sacrifices."

"You don't actually sacrifice your friends!" Anna shouted.

"I was only friends with her because I had to be. So technically, I'm not." As she raised her hand, a finger fell off, plopping onto her science textbook. She quickly scooped it up with her other hand and stuck it back on. "Look, I can text Tabitha to meet us here after school."

"No," Anna said. "We'll meet outside the cafeteria."

"Yes, outside," Eden agreed.

"Fine, whatever. We'll meet outside the cafeteria after school. Then you can tell her what you did to her, and I can help put her out of her misery."

CHAPTER 34

ANNA

Harper was falling apart right in front of them. "Give it up, Harper," Anna urged. "You don't have a choice anymore."

"What?" Harper reached up to touch her ear. It was barely hanging on.

"It will be easier for you to just let go," Anna said softly.

Harper had only one leg left to stand on. Her left one. Her right leg was lying on the ground next to Eden.

"It doesn't have to be that way." Harper looked at her hands sadly as her fingers fell off, one at a time.

But this time she couldn't reattach them. They shattered, turning into dust as they hit the ground. The rings from her fingers made clinking sounds against each other as they fell.

"It does," Anna said, with more passion. "I know how badly you want to live. But you can't. Not anymore."

Eden watched with wide eyes, not saying a word.

"I can find another body."

Anna shook her head. "It doesn't work like that."

"But it did before."

"Huh?" Eden said.

Anna's mouth fell open. "What?"

"My old body, my Harper Sweety body, was sick. Not sick as in hot, but, like, really sick. I was in the hospital and the next thing I remember was looking down at myself. I didn't understand what was happening. I went screaming for help. And that's when I saw Mary. She was in one of the hospital rooms too. I was scared and . . ." Harper's bottom lip began to tremble. "I jumped into her body. It was like a force pulled me toward her."

Anna gasped. "You took her body?"

"Yes," Harper whispered as she lost her balance and sat down on the ground. Her foot fell over to the side.

"But she tried to fight me, which only made me want her body more."

"She was *alive*?" Eden threw a hand over her mouth.

"Well, yeah." She looked up. All sadness was gone. "She tried to push me out, but she was weak. I was angry and it made me stronger. You know, what doesn't kill you makes you stronger," Harper chuckled. "And it was so easy. I climbed into her hospital bed and pushed her. Just a little bit. And her spirit was pushed outside her body. Once I claimed it, she was even weaker. She didn't stand a chance of surviving. Not against me, anyway."

Anna shook her head. She couldn't believe what Harper was saying. Anna glanced at her phone. Mary. The ghost that claimed she'd lost her body. She quickly sent a text on her phone.

"Is that why you were so eager to get your—I mean *her* body back?" Anna asked. "Because you knew Mary's spirit would be looking for you?"

Harper nodded. "Why else would I want to live the life of a poor girl?"

The air in front of them shimmered.

"Didn't you ever think that Mary might have been the one who pushed you off the balcony?" Anna asked. "You'll eventually have to see her. So just let go. Let go and move on." Anna tried to stay calm.

"I just need a little more time. If I can find another body . . . someone who is weak or—"

The words died on Harper's lips. Her facial features froze and the rest of her body went limp. Eden and Anna watched helplessly as Harper's body slowly disintegrated in front of their eyes.

"Um." Eden turned to Anna. "Did that really just happen?"

Anna nodded. It was over.

"What happened?" Tabitha strolled up and stood beside them. "Eww, what is that?" She pointed to a small pile of ashes on the ground.

Anna and Eden exchanged glances. When nobody answered her, Tabitha looked between the two girls. "What? What is it? And where's Harper? She told me to meet her here. She said she could help me with these really bad headaches I've been having."

"It's a long story," Anna said.

CHAPTER 35

ANNA

The overwhelming scent of lemons arrived just moments before Lucy did. She looked down at the pile of ashes and sadly shook her head. "That's too bad. I really had high hopes for her."

"I knew you were behind this!" Anna shouted, pointing her finger inches from Lucy's face.

"Who are you yelling at, Anna?" Tabitha asked, taking a step back.

"Go ahead, tell your sweet stepsister all about me," Lucy said with a smirk.

Eden gently elbowed Anna. "I'm guessing you're yelling at Lucy but nobody else can see her." She nodded in Tabitha's direction.

Anna's eyes darted nervously between Lucy and

Tabitha. It was what she wanted—to freak Tabitha out. But something was holding her back.

"I see you're still terrific at making decisions," Lucy pointed out. "Maybe I should help you with that."

Eden pointed at Lucy's now visible form. "It *is* Lucy!" She turned to Anna. "This is way creepier than I imagined. You know, since I knew her before."

"It's great to see you too, Eden." Lucy didn't hold back her disgust.

"I don't get it, Lucy!" Anna was furious with the ghost. "Why did you come back and why did you do this"—she made a sweeping motion over the ashes—"to Harper?"

"Obviously this isn't how it was supposed to end." Lucy folded her arms, hovering a few inches higher. "She either didn't do it in time or she lost her nerve. I shouldn't be surprised either way."

"Why don't you tell us how it *was* supposed to end, then, Lucy? Because you're still not making any sense," Anna said.

"Yeah, tell us," echoed Eden.

"It was supposed to end with Harper taking over a living body." Lucy pointed at Tabitha. "Yours, to be exact."

"What?" Tabitha crinkled her nose. "My body?"

"But then you had to go and eat that stupid cupcake,"

Lucy continued. "Which led to the whole brain thing, and so you turned out to be totally useless. So we had to switch to plan B."

"And plan B was . . . ?" Anna wanted her to just spit it out.

"It was you, Anna. I'm surprised you haven't figured that out by now. She was going to kick you out and take control of your body."

"And what would've happened to Anna?" Eden asked.

"She would've been forced to live just like me. As a wandering spirit."

"Yeah, we could've been the best ghoul friends ever," Anna said, frowning.

Eden shook her head. "It still doesn't add up. Why did you even need a living body?"

Lucy glared at Anna. "To get Johnny back, of course."

"Are we really back to this?" Anna yelled. "Because that's so three months ago!"

"Well, if you had just done what I wanted you to the first time, then I wouldn't have to still deal with this."

Anna noticed Tabitha backing farther away. She looked as if she might break into a sprint at any moment. Maybe even back to New York.

"Let us explain, Tabitha," Anna said, taking a step toward her.

"No, no, no." Tabitha shook her head back and forth. She stumbled, then fell to her knees, groaning in pain.

"Do something!" Anna shouted at Eden. They were just about out of time.

"Yeah, do something," Lucy said, laughing.

Eden looked at Anna. "You know I can't. I'm not strong enough."

"You could at least try, Eden," Anna said. "Maybe you're stronger than you realize. But you have to try. . . ."

Eden ran to Tabitha's side, placing her hands on Tabitha's while closing her eyes tightly and muttering words Anna couldn't understand. But Tabitha's cries grew louder. "Make it stop!" she sobbed.

"I'm . . . trying. . . ." Eden's grip on Tabitha tightened as she chanted faster.

Anna stood next to Eden. "C'mon. I know you can do this—" Her words cut off when she noticed Eden's nose was bleeding.

"Oh no," Anna whispered as she realized what was happening. "This is hurting you."

Another pair of hands reached out for Tabitha. "I can help."

"Archer!" Anna had never been so happy to see him. Like Eden, Archer closed his eyes, placing his hands over Eden's, and began mumbling. Each minute felt like an eternity. Eden's voice became quieter until it was nothing more than a whisper. The air around them grew thick. A loud crack followed by a bright burst of light jolted Anna as Archer broke away and Eden collapsed.

A slight breeze ruffled Anna's hair as Millie materialized. "Oh my God! Is she okay?"

"Please tell me she's only unconscious and didn't, you know, bite the dust." Lucy hovered over Eden's body as Archer held her hand.

"What do you care?" Millie snapped.

"I don't. I need to prepare myself if I have to deal with her in the afterlife."

As if on cue, Eden came to and Archer helped her to slowly sit up.

"You're okay!" Anna hugged her friend. "I didn't know this could hurt you. I swear. I'm so sorry. For everything."

"No, I'm sorry." Eden coughed. "I shouldn't have done a spell on you."

"I know you were only trying to help. But none of that matters anymore. I'm just glad you're okay."

Tabitha groaned, holding the side of her head. She ran her hand over a small bump, wincing.

"Are you all right?" Eden asked.

Tabitha nodded, a dazed look on her face. "It still hurts. But not from the headaches. Not like before."

"It worked. We did it." Archer winked at Eden.

"I'm still confused about what happened," Tabitha said.

"It's a long story," Anna explained. "But it started when you ate that cupcake meant for Johnny."

"Yeah, I guess it was around that time." Tabitha thought for a moment. "Do you think it was a gluten allergy or something?"

"Or something." Lucy snorted.

"I wonder if Johnny got headaches like I did," Tabitha said.

Eden and Anna exchanged looks. "Why would he?" Eden asked suspiciously.

"Because if the cupcake caused that, then maybe it did something to Johnny too."

Hope suddenly shot through Anna. "I thought Johnny didn't eat the cupcake."

"He didn't. Not really. But he did swipe a finger of frosting and sprinkles," Tabitha said.

"He did? What color were the sprinkles?" Anna fired off.

"What? How would I know?" Tabitha gave Anna a weird look.

Eden leaned in to Anna. "He could have regained a few specific memories. This could be good!"

"Or very bad," Anna whispered back. "Depending on which memories."

Millie cleared her throat. "Speaking of memories,

remember that night in the cemetery with the Ouija board?"

"You mean the night you disappeared on us?"

"Yeah. Where did you go?" Eden asked.

"I tried to get to your dad before we lost the connection completely."

"And?" Anna could feel her heart beat faster.

Millie looked down, shaking her head. "Sorry. I tried to find him. I really did."

"Thanks for trying." Anna meant it, although she couldn't help feeling disappointment settle over her.

"Maybe I can help with that too." Archer took Anna's phone, clicked through it while mumbling something, then handed it back to her.

Anna searched through her phone. A box popped up saying "new update installed." "What is this?"

"It's an update that gives you access to some really useful apps."

"Oh, like our Spell Phones?" Eden asked.

"Kind of. Except her access is more . . . ghost-friendly."

"There's an app called the Spirit Seeker?" Anna looked up.

"Yep." Archer smiled. "Contact any spirit you wish. It might take a while for some to get back to you."

"Wow." Anna could hardly believe it. It sounded so

easy. Maybe even a little too easy. "Wait a minute. So you mean this whole time, all I needed was an app? On my phone?"

. . .

Lucy had disappeared after that day, but Anna doubted it was permanent. Too bad she didn't have an app for a spirit zapper. After explaining everything, Tabitha didn't go running back to New York like Anna had originally hoped. Who would've guessed that her new stepsister was a believer in all the paranormal? Sharing secrets brought them closer, and they were actually able to tolerate each other while in the same room. Anna was even excited about volunteering together at the teen help line.

Anna used the Spirit Seeker app to contact her dad. She was still waiting to hear from him. She was a little nervous thinking about actually communicating with him. Now she needed to contact Mary. She still hadn't heard back from her, and now that her body was a pile of ashes, her only choice was to cross over. Unless she was the vengeful type and was looking for Harper.

Eden definitely seemed happier with Archer around. He and Johnny were also becoming fast friends. The only downside to Archer being so powerful was the bad news that came with it. He broke the news to Anna and Tabitha that there was a spell on their parents. Which would really explain a lot. But because neither of them was familiar with dark magic—which was where the spell came from—they couldn't break it. Not until they could find the source of the spell. Which only meant something evil was lurking in their tiny town of Winchester Village. And for once, it wasn't Lucy.

Anna's phone buzzed with a new text. She smiled. It was from Johnny. He could still make her blush, even over the phone. They were meeting up later. Johnny had regained memories of when Anna first moved to town, so they were spending a lot more time together.

Everything was going to be okay. Well, minus the whole spell thing with her parents. But she'd worry about that later. For now, she wanted to hold on to this happy feeling and pretend, even if only for a moment, that things were finally falling into place instead of falling to pieces.

"Ready?" Tabitha poked her head into Anna's room. Today was their first day volunteering at the teen help line together.

"Ready!" Anna scooped up her bag and slung it over her shoulder.

She was actually excited to start helping. And

Johnny would be there too. But that wasn't the reason she wanted to volunteer. Okay, maybe a little bit. But she also felt that if she could help dead people, she could easily help the living.

After all, how hard could it be?

ACKNOWLEDGMENTS

Many thanks to all the wonderful people who helped bring this book to life:

As always, my astounding agent, Rosemary Stimola, and extraordinary editor, Wendy Loggia. And a huge thank-you to the amazing team at Penguin Random House.

Angela and Emma Sweeney, your support, friendship, and inspiration mean the world to me. I can't wait for the day when I can walk (or gracefully trip) into a bookstore and see Emma's book on the shelf!

Amie Borst, I can't imagine writing anything without you! You inspire creativity when least expected but most welcomed.

My family and friends, for your unconditional love and support and unlimited supply of (what else?) chocolate!

ABOUT THE AUTHOR

Rose Cooper is the author/illustrator of *Gossip from the Girls' Room, Rumors from the Boys' Room, Secrets from the Sleeping Bag,* and *I Text Dead People.*

When Rose was a teenager, she moved to a tiny town where her stepdad was a mortician, her mom was a corpse cosmetician, and their house was on cemetery grounds. She lives in Sacramento, California, with her family and makes sure all her texts are to the living.

Visit her at Rose-Cooper.com.

Follow Rose Cooper on